"In the battle against conventional wisdom,
artistic expression is our greatest weapon."

– The Artist formally known as Sun Tzu

WARPAINT

BOLD, UNUSUAL AND PROVOCATIVE WORKS
FROM AROUND THE WORLD

Issue 1, Print Edition
June 2012

Issue 1, Print Edition - June 2012

Editor-in-chief: Corey King

Volume Editor: Bev Sandell Greenberg

Managing Editor: Danielle King

Cover Art: Ben Clarkson

ISBN 978-0-9878577-1-2

Contact: warpaint@zenfri.com

Submit: submit@zenfri.com

Follow us @warwithpaint

Like us on Facebook.com/warwithpaint

Table of Contents

War With Paint

This is the first issue of what I hope will become a biannual anthology of unusual and thought provoking creative works. I went into this project with more passion than sense, but now that you finally have this issue in your hands, I can say with confidence that I'm proud of what we have accomplished.

With *Warpaint*, we set out to create a place where the rebels, misfits and unconventional thinkers can tell their stories. This first issue draws a line in the sand, preparing us to do battle with conventional wisdom. This confrontation does not stem from a desire to protest everything that has stood the test of time, but from a belief that without experiments of the mind, we can never know for certain what is right, just and true. That is why nothing is sacred in *Warpaint*. Not even the beliefs and ideals of the editors.

We are 100% artist run and artist funded. We don't solicit grants, seek out advertisers or consult with investors. Our resources are the blood, sweat and tears of our staff and the submissions of over 200 artists worldwide who seek little more than a safe haven for their bold, unusual or provocative work. Submitters ranged from award-winning, nationally recognized writers and visual artists, to those who are being published for the first time in this issue.

Every purchased copy of *Warpaint* will have its revenue divided evenly amongst the contributors. This means that as the publisher, we make as much or as little as every other name that graces these pages.

Come what may, we're all in the trenches together.

For this reason, I encourage contributors, readers and artists to join the discussion on our Facebook and Twitter pages. And of course, if you have something bold, unusual or provocative to say, we welcome your work.

Thank you for reading *Warpaint*. May the world find you well in the battle ahead.

Corey King

Editor-in-chief

BEAUTIFUL INSANITY

Julianna Kozma

Scratch!

A match grated against the rough cement wall and hissed to life. A blinding flame suddenly exploded in the dark, simpering down to a mere flicker seconds later. The surrounding walls, damp and cold, weighed down on the flame, seeming to suffocating its feeble will to burn.

A boy gently held the match and cupped it against an invisible draft. His hands shook from the cold as he fumbled to light a stubby candle on a table. It cast a weak glow on the numerous objects scattered on the pockmarked wooden surface. He took the candle and walked over to a deep recess in the wall. He bent, knees cracking, and used the candle to light a fire. Within minutes, the flames licked the crumpled paper and brittle sticks. He stood back and stared at the fire, satisfied.

After a minute more, the boy returned to his work. An hour later, he sat back, laid down his tools, and admired his work.

Not bad, he thought. *Perhaps a bit more colour over here. And that part could use a drop of glitter. There. That's it. All done.*

The boy straightened and backed away from the table. His pale face shone with a feverish intensity. He sighed. He was tired. It had been an extremely long night, but he still wasn't finished.

He packed up his tools and shoved them in a moldy cupboard. He picked up the candle and shuffled over to some wooden crates stacked in one corner of his workshop. Bending, he held the candle over the crates. Ten large batteries, their metallic contacts poking through black plastic casings, lay nestled within the tight confines of the wooden boxes. He carefully checked the levels of each battery and frowned. Battery number eight was getting low again. He'd have to have a look at it once he got back.

From another dark corner of his underground hovel, the boy wrestled with a hand trolley until it finally gave up its hold. The rusty wheels creaked and groaned when pushed towards the table. He had to oil the thing every night on account of the dampness, but he had run out of grease yesterday. He had the raw materials he needed to render more grease, but not tonight. No time.

The boy carefully eased a large object off the table and managed to get it onto the trolley without dropping it. As he bent to strap the object onto the trolley, he noticed the wires snaking out of the object. It was still hooked up to the batteries.

Damn! Forgot to unplug it.

The boy wiped his damp hands on his overalls. He shook his head, but then bent to work, fighting with the wires and finally managing to pull the plugs out. Carefully, he wheeled the trolley towards a recessed door, flipped the latch open and went out, pulling the strong metal door closed behind him. Flickering torches lit a narrow hallway along which ran several doors. Just as he passed the third door to his right, it opened suddenly.

"Were you waiting for me?" he asked, startled.

"Yes." A young girl, no more than thirteen, stood in the doorway, holding another candle. She was wearing the same outfit as the boy, uniforms for the job.

The boy squinted, trying to look past the girl. "Have you finished with yours?"

"An hour ago. This was only a repair and it still had some juice. "

"Lucky you. Mine was completely dead. I had to start from scratch." The boy shook his head. "Come on. Let's head out before daylight. We need to set these in place before everyone wakes."

The girl frowned, but then nodded her head. Moments later, she was pushing her own fully loaded trolley down the hallway, right behind the boy.

At the end of the hall was an ancient freight elevator. The boy reached out and pushed a button. He glanced over at the girl's trolley while they waited.

"You did a great job, Marie," he said. "Still looks almost real."

"Thanks. This one's a real old one too, but you can't tell, can you?" Marie stood back and admired the object on her trolley.

"How old do you think it is?"

Marie cocked her head to the side, considering the question. "Hard to say. This one has no visitors anymore, so I can't ask anybody. But I've been working on it for at least three years."

Three years? The boy was shocked. *Three years?* He thought they only lasted about a year at the most. *Three years is too long!*

The girl saw the boy's distress. "Don't you want it to last forever?"

The boy paled. "That's insane."

"Some people think it's beautiful." Marie gently ran her fingers across the boy's hand and smiled wistfully as he quickly snatched it away. "If it were you, what would you want?"

Before the boy could answer, the elevator came to a stop at their feet. They carefully maneuvered their trolleys inside, swallowed by the sudden darkness. Marie reached out and groped for the button just off to her left. As soon as she pushed it, the doors clanked shut and the elevator's motor started up again. Through the clanking and sputtering of the ancient contraption, the boy heard Marie swallow.

"You could turn it on if you want some light," he suggested. He could *feel* her nervousness.

"No…that's okay. I want to conserve its energy."

"But it'll only be for a minute –"

"No. Really. I'm fine. It's about time I get used to the dark. I mean, look at where we live. Ironic that we're called lighters, don't you think?"

The boy remained silent.

"Besides, if I turn it on, it would feel almost like abuse. And disrespect."

Despite Marie's soft sing-song voice, the soothing words penetrated the boy's silence, and he snorted in frustration. "Disrespect? But that's what it does. It lights up. That's its purpose."

"No. It's not. It's meant to comfort, and ease people's pain."

The boy shook his head, but then realized Marie could not see him. He cleared his throat. "I agree about the respect part, but people should forget and move on. It's not healthy to dwell on something that's gone."

Marie just smiled. "Beautiful insanity. Hard to know what's right and what's wrong."

The boy bristled. "I'm already ten and I've been doing this for almost a year. I know lots, especially right from wrong."

"Yeah, you know lots about technical stuff. And I agree that you're a brilliant perfectionist and your final works are breathtaking. But when you get out on top, you don't stick around, do you? When everyone is there, admiring your work, you leave before sun up, so no one sees you. One day you should stay. Hide behind one of those old stones. And listen. Then I think you'll know your real purpose. I think you'll understand a bit better and see. There are no easy answers."

The boy remained silent. What did Marie know? But then he grimaced. Talk was that she'd been at this since the age of five, so he guessed she knew quite a bit. Still, this talk about purpose was disturbing and unexpected.

The elevator finally came to a screeching halt and the rickety doors wheezed open. Marie and the boy wheeled their trolleys through another hallway that led directly outside.

It was still dark, just the way the boy liked it. Mount Royal, in the heart of Montreal, was eerily quiet. The moon was out, almost full, and brimming with a cold, pale light, shafts of white lit up the narrow paved pathways. The children wove their way around grassy knolls and hillocks. They never came across another soul. It was always like that at night.

Ten minutes into their walk, they came to a fork in the road.

"I'll meet you back here in twenty," said the boy. Marie nodded and turned left. The boy veered off in the other direction.

The trolley's squeaky wheels creaked and groaned as he pushed it forward. He loved to meander through the park at night. The artificial grass artfully covered the dead earth, and plastic pine trees sparkled with a vitality seldom seen in the past, when there were real trees. Even the air smelled fresher, somewhat less metallic. This area of the park was his part of the world. Marie had her own sector to take care of, as did Ralph, Charlie, Louanne, Sophie and Chelsea. There were others, but he didn't know them all that well. Many in this business came and went. The pay was great, but the conditions were less than human.

Before he knew it, he came to the spot he had marked yesterday. It was well back from the main pathways, almost hidden behind a small copse of silk and vinyl weeping willows. The boy thought it almost peaceful, a place veiled against the real world. A smile tickled the corners of his mouth and then he laughed.

The sound, so alien in its simplicity, and so rare, shocked him. Suddenly feeling overwhelmed, the boy hung his head. And saw the flowers. Those were new. He bent to get a better look. The deep red petals looked almost black in the moonlight. The boy reached out and hesitantly poked them with a shaky finger.

"Real!" He jerked his finger back as if burnt. "Since when does anyone have real flowers?"

Thoughts exploded simultaneously in his head, leaving him shaken. The boy clumsily stood up. He nervously scanned his surroundings. What if whoever had left the flowers was still here? But everything was still. Not even the sighing of the wind disturbed the night. But his calm was shattered by a bundle of petals.

Abruptly, he turned back towards the trolley and quickly set to work. Within a couple of minutes, the object he had trundled from within the bowels of the earth was placed in its place of honour. The boy stood and once again gazed at his work. This time he didn't feel the same satisfaction of a job well done.

As he stared at the object, he felt his eyes being pulled downwards. He fought the urge, but lost. His eyes floated to the flowers on the ground. And he remembered Marie's question.

"Don't you want it to last longer?" she had asked him.

"No," he whispered. "I don't want it to last a single minute. This is *wrong*."

He grabbed the trolley and rushed back through the park, passing other objects of various sizes and shapes, but all similar to the one he had abandoned near the fake willows. All similar except for one glaring fact; these were lit up. The boy had forgotten to turn his on!

The boy grabbed his hair in bunched fists. *No, no, no!*

But he had to go back. He had to turn it on. It was part of the contract.

After what seemed like an eternity, he dropped his hands and reluctantly turned back the way he had come. Leaving his trolley behind, the boy hurried towards the copse of willows. As he rounded the final bend that led around the trees, the boy pulled up short.

Standing in front of the object he had just installed was a woman. He watched in shock as she bent over and reached behind the object's base. With a snap, a brilliant light poured from the object, bathing the woman in its harsh glow. She cried out and stumbled, but managed not to fall. However, her sudden movement forced her to turn, and her gaze fell right on the boy, freezing him in place.

A heartbeat passed. Slowly, the woman raised her hand and gestured toward the object. "Are you the one who did this? You're the lighter, aren't you? What's your name?"

He was off, running recklessly through the park. His feet and heart pounded loudly. Marie was already waiting for him at the fork. Without another word, he grabbed her hand and pulled her along with him, only stopping once they were back at the elevator.

"What's wrong?" she asked breathlessly.

"We need to get inside and back down," he hissed. He flung open the elevator doors and dragged Marie inside. The boy stabbed at the control button; within seconds, they were moving back down, deep into the earth.

Marie's voice reached out through the inky blackness. "What happened?"

"She saw me!" the boy wailed.

"Who did?"

"The *client*! She was there. She's not supposed to be there. Not at night. No one goes out at night. Not anymore."

Marie was quiet for a while. "Sometimes they do. Especially when the experience is still new. They don't know what else to do, and try to reach out. Even to us. Did you talk to her?"

The boy was aghast. "No! Of course not. We're not allowed."

Marie sighed. "That's not true."

"But Ralph told me not to go near them."

Marie frowned, her small face puckered. "That's just resentment from our kind. You *are* allowed to talk to them. I think that talking to them makes us human, rather than the monsters we appear to be, even sometimes to ourselves."

The boy looked unconvinced.

"Did she say anything?" Marie asked. "To you, I mean."

"Yeah," the boy's voice quavered. "She asked me my name."

Marie fell silent again. The elevator finally came to a lurching halt and Marie flung open the gated door. She turned to face the boy. The narrow hallway was still lit by the torches and the flickering glow warmly shadowed her tired young face. "Was that so wrong?"

"*Yessss!*" hissed the boy, wringing his hands. "She's one of *them!* They should never know me."

Marie laid a gentle hand on the boy's arm. "What about us, then? Should we know you?"

"What?" The boy was startled, and backed away from her touch. Marie dropped her hand.

"What *is* your name?"

The boy was speechless. His name! Twice, in one night!

He shook his head. No! He couldn't. Not even for Marie.

Marie smiled sadly. "Maybe later." She patted him on the arm and opened her door. "Good night."

The boy watched his friend enter her room and close the door behind her. God, he was tired. Drained. The work was hard enough, but now this. . .

The next night started with a loud bang. A door was slammed and the boy awoke with a start. Seconds later, someone was pounding on his door.

"Heard about last night." Ralph, red-headed and filthy, stood outside in the shadowed hallway. "Marie told me. You did the right thing, though. Never talk to them. We need to keep our distance, you know."

The boy rubbed his eyes, still dazed from sleep. "Where's Marie?"

"Out. No contracts tonight, so no work for us," Ralph grimaced. "Bet she's people watching. But I think she's finding that harder and harder to do. Have you noticed it's been quieter here of late? Even on top. Less and less people sticking around."

"Maybe they've managed to beat this thing."

Ralph scratched his head. "Maybe, but that's bad news for us. What'll we do then? We'll be out of work."

Good question, thought the boy. What will he do with his time? Live on top? This was the only life he remembered, and his skill as a lighter was all he knew how to do. This was his life and it was adequate.

Then he flashed to the woman from last night and cold fingers of doubt tickled his soul. Who was right, Marie or Ralph? She was up on top, and Ralph was down below. Both were doing what they thought was right. And what was he doing?

The boy turned from Ralph and went into the bathroom, slamming the door behind him. Several hours later he shuffled out. Ralph was gone. Of course he would be, thought the boy. He puttered around the workshop area, cleaning up the mess from the night before. Then he fixed himself something to eat. Later on he tried fixing the dying battery, but realized he'd need Ralph's help to render the materials into the oil needed to get the juice back up. So many things to do and so busy. It was good.

Yet the thought continued to nibble at his heart, like picking at a scab. Marie was up with *them*. Watching. Yearning. Maybe even connecting. Suddenly, the glass in his hand went flying across the workshop, shattering against the damp walls that wept with moisture.

"Connections are wrong!" he groaned, doubling over, hands on his knees, muttering. "Marie is wrong. Ralph is wrong. No names...no names ... no names."

He grabbed a ratty coat off a chair and left his room. Before he realized where he was going, the elevator ground to a halt and he was outside. He tilted his head back and gasped. Another clear night. The moon and stars cast shadows across the green expanse of fakeness. He looked around his surroundings. No Marie. Running, he came to the park's exit. Still no Marie. Could she have ventured out? Not only up, but actually out?

The boy shivered. He couldn't do it. He couldn't follow her. He couldn't leave. He walked over to the black wrought iron gates and leaned against one of the cold posts. Slowly, he sank down to the ground. He'd wait for her here, he decided, but within the hour, he was asleep.

Bright morning light beat down on his pale face, jerking him awake. He frantically grabbed the metal post. Where was he? Outside! And it was morning. To his horror, he realized people would be coming. He got back on his feet and quickly left the gate, looking neither left nor right. Finally, after several awful minutes, he was back in the safety of the elevator and blessed darkness.

In the hallway, just steps from his door, Ralph stood talking to a girl called Sophie. The boy was too far away to hear what Ralph was saying, but it must have been a joke since Sophie was laughing.

"Hey man, where the hell were you?" Ralph started in as soon as he spied the approaching boy. "We've been looking for you. You've got a job, and it's got to be done well. We all voted and decided you'd be the best. No one here would do it justice."

"Who's it for?" mumbled the boy.

"That woman you did the job for the other day. Highly unusual. Never had this happen to us before. I mean, never had someone from above pay a contract for anyone from below. You're on your own on this. Just show us the final result before you set it in place. That's the deal. The papers are inside."

Before the boy could respond, Ralph and Sophie left, entering one of the many hallway doors. The boy was still dazed from finding himself exposed to daylight, so he had hardly paid attention to what Ralph had said. The word contract filtered in, but thoughts of Marie still occupied his mind.

Once inside his room, he picked up the papers on the counter, glanced through the map and then turned on the batteries, warming them up for the job ahead. He went to one of the cupboards, started taking out his tools and apron and arranged them on a nearby workbench. Satisfied that everything was in order, he finally approached the table. The object was already there, ready for his transformation.

"Hmmm. One of the small ones," he mumbled, then sighed. "A harder job."

He lit another candle and bent down for a closer look. His hand froze for an instant and then started trembling, the flame waving erratically in the cold air. His breath came in gasps and his heart thundered, shattered by the sight. The boy jerked away from the table and fled to a dark corner of the room, dropping the candle. The weak flame hissed as it went out.

He wasn't sure how long he had cowered in the corner, anguishing. But somewhere within his haze, a decision had been made. He moved around in a daze. A contract was a contract, after all. The work had to be done. With mechanical brilliance, he worked non-stop, honoring the object at hand. Throughout the day and well into the night, he continued. Ralph came to visit a few times, nodding and congratulating, but the boy paid no attention. By midnight, the work was done. The boy wrestled the trolley out of the corner and gently placed the object on it.

"Oh Marie, you should see what I've done!" he whispered. He grabbed the map and left his room, pushing the trolley ahead of him. He was about to knock on Marie's door, but then dropped his hand.

Outside again. This time, the moon hid behind a low bank of clouds, but at least there was no rain. He glanced at his map, and then, head down, proceeded along one of the numerous paths. Soon he was at the spot marked by the contract writers.

The woman was already waiting, the same woman he had run from only the night before, or was it a lifetime ago. He wasn't sure. She watched in silence as he set about installing the object on the newly formed pedestal. The boy plugged it in to the base, and then flicked the switch. A dazzling beam of pure light illuminated the grounds and shot through the clouds.

Heads tilted back, the boy and the woman gazed up at the sky.

"She's a star," whispered the woman. "None of the others are as brilliant as she is. You did an exceptional job."

The boy remained silent, tears coursing down his cheeks.

The woman turned and looked at him. "She was my friend. Did you know? Did she tell you? We've met every night for the past few weeks. Sometimes she would stay with me at my house, especially near the end when I was losing him. I think that's how she got sick. But she never told me. She never let me see that she got the same disease as my husband. I could have helped her."

The boy shook his head, but the woman grabbed his hands, beseeching, pleading.

"Yes. We have the medicine now and it works on most people. She knew that," the woman cried, but then dropped her hands. "But she couldn't leave you. She said she knew you were one of the special ones destined to migrate to the top, here with us, but you weren't ready yet. And she thought she could keep the disease at bay."

The boy was confused. "Why would she think that?"

The woman smiled down at the boy, the same way Marie had just a couple of days ago. "Because she had hope."

The boy looked at the woman. "She wanted me to live out here? On top? Why would she think I would want that?"

Again, the woman smiled. "Because you cared."

The woman saw the boy was still confused and tried to explain. "You told Marie that we need to move on. That making these objects last two, three or more years was unhealthy. Many of your kind don't even think about what you're doing. Emotionally distant. I understand that it helps you from going insane. But you started to question all this."

Yes, the boy remembered. But he was still puzzled. "Then why make me do this?" he asked, gesturing at the glowing object.

"It was her last wish. She said you would know what to do."

The boy turned and faced the light.

Marie, encased in clear polymer, smiled at him. Her eyes sparkled with the warmth of life although she was dead. The woman was right. He had done a great job, his best ever. After all, it was Marie. He had used all the techniques she had taught him, embalming her with that special luminous concoction he had worked months on to perfect. The polymer clear coat was blended to perfection, the preservative elements within it chemically enhanced to last years, as long as power was maintained. She was now impervious to rain and snow, cold or heat. She would last forever. He had made sure of that. It was important to do a good job.

"My name is Chloe," said the woman. "Whenever you're ready, you can come and see me. I will help you get back into this world. Marie wanted this. Whenever you are ready. . ."

The boy stood there, gazing at his dear friend. Really, his only friend. No one else cared for him like she did. He stared at Marie while the woman beside him shared his grief.

Slowly, he approached Marie. He reached out a hand and ever so gently, caressed her cheek. The smooth plastic coating was sleek but cold. No life breath warmed his hand as he traced the contours of her smile, and no laugh broke the silence. She would never touch him again.

With a sigh, he dropped to his knees, reached behind Marie's statue, and flicked off the switch, plunging Marie into darkness. He knew the others would take care of her. Whether they would bury her, as was the custom with their own, or leave her lit up was not his decision. The contract was fulfilled. He stood and looked at Marie one last time.

"My name is Joshua."

Memorial Tree No.XIV

Gerard Lange

XIV

Teeth as Eyes saw Aida, Unafraid

Keith Kennedy

She knew how wrong it was. But less than a fortnight ago, Aida had come through the ritual of womanhood with an acuteness of desire never before felt. Sure, she had always been restless, even rebellious. But now, as a woman, that sword had become sharp and deadly. It had not, however, turned its gleaming point in the direction of the many male suitors of her village; no, it had turned toward exploration of a different kind, a simpler kind.

And so, that morning – despite knowing it was forbidden – Aida took one of her father's many boats and set out to discover once and for all what was on the other side of the lake.

The fog was dense and low, but she had decided it was the day, and would not let nature stop her. It always abated before midday and as she approached the far bank, the sun was high, and the fog dispersed on schedule.

Shortly after disembarking, she noticed the first substantial feature of the hilly terrain. Not far from where the sand of the beach became pale grass, there was a worn area and a dark patch in a small hillock. She approached with caution, expectation a whale in her gullet, and as she closed the distance, the dark patch in the hill revealed itself to be a sealed aperture. It was driftwood, dark and stained with the season's heavy rains, fashioned into a doorway. Beyond, beneath the hillock lay a domicile of unknown occupation.

Aida stopped and looked around, quelling her brazenness. She turned south and traveled along the edge of the grass, then climbed up the hill and stood above the assumed home, looking westward over the rolling grass. There was no one to be seen. Far off, just at the edge of her vision, a line of deep emerald trees marked the boundary of a sizeable forest. She scanned the edge of the trees carefully, but saw no movement.

Returning to the door, having convinced herself that the small home's resident was present, she stomped her feet and cleared her throat until certain that she'd made significant ruckus to alert of her presence. But nothing happened. Assuming the inhabitant asleep, she was faced with a moral dilemma. Before long, her decision abruptly made, she was easing her weight onto the door. She had not paddled alone across the lake for nothing.

As it turned out, the door needed to be pulled to be opened. She took her fingers and wedged them between two pieces of damp driftwood and pulled back, first carefully and then more sharply until the door came loose of the dirt at its base. It made little noise, but she remained still for a long while afraid of having awoken the occupant.

There was again no immediate consequence, so she continued. The door opened more easily now, and she brought it along until a little light settled into the open space beyond. There was a packed dirt floor, but no other discernible features. She poked her head inside, but the light only traversed the floor for so long before bashing hard against a wall of darkness. With her head still inside, she pushed the door further ajar with her outstretched foot, bracing herself against the hill with her hand until the sun traced a perfect silhouette of her on the floor. Now she could see most of the room. The walls were hung with simple and familiar things: tools for catching, cleaning and gathering. Against the far wall was a piece of wood atop four other pieces, stacked to resemble a sheep.

How silly, Aida thought, as she eased the door open ever further, her foot now raised a good ways off the ground to accommodate the rearward extension. In this strange position, her hand – having created too much pressure on the dirt of the doorframe – dislodged a chunk of grass and soil, loosing her to tumble face first onto the ground.

Any doubt about the hovel being occupied was now completely dispersed; she rose, no longer feeling the need to be careful and forcefully pushed the door all the way open. Light flooded in, nestling deep into the corners of the earth where it could do the most good. At the far end of the room there was a pile of bedding, some dried grass, a mound of animal skins and a blanket the likes of which she'd never seen. It was sewn together and woven like a basket from what seemed to be large, leathery skins.

She moved toward it, assuming the altered light at her back was caused by the door closing on its own. A strange grunt, a human sound, told her otherwise and she instinctively, yet quietly threw herself forward, rolling to the ground and whipping a handful of furs over her body. She pulled her knees up to her torso, and in this position, completely covered by the skins, tried to breathe without sound.

The tiny sound of cautious footsteps penetrated the fur of the animal's hide and reached her fear-sharpened ears. She traced the sounds, heard the man enter his little home and stand, examining the area. She felt momentary relief when he didn't come directly for her. He had alerted her from outside, probably having stopped to wonder why his door was ajar.

Slowly he moved deeper into the place. He stopped beside her, planting his foot so close that a small piece of straw he trod upon rose from the ground, its other end poking her in the nose beneath the furs. She held her breath and prayed she wouldn't sneeze.

After an eon of intense listening and stillness from both parties, the man turned and left, quickly and with purpose. She heard him return; not long after that, the light peaking in beneath her blankets was diffused. She listened as he performed some sort of task near the door. Then, after a time, she realized there was no more noise.

It took her some effort, but Aida finally built the courage to peak from beneath her hiding place. He must not be inside with her, or she would hear him. Either that or he would have come to his bed. Still, she feared that, when she raised the fur, he would be sitting, cross-legged before her, spear in hand, ready to kill the intruder.

Having built the vision too long in her head, she raised the blanket slowly and involuntarily shut her eyes, waiting for the kill shot to come. But it didn't. Exhaling, she opened her eyes and saw only the darkness of the hovel, the tools and weapons on the wall barely visible by the light sifting in through the closed door.

Gathering courage, she raised the blanket further and brought herself out from under the skins and to her feet. She was alone inside, but where was the man? Had he vanished into the seeming nothing from whence he'd appeared? Or was he just outside, waiting to see if the opener-of-doors would return?

She was now frightened by a new vision of reprisal, one where she opened the door and the spear blow came from above where the man was waiting atop the hillock. She moved quickly to the wall of tools and selected a wicked looking stone knife, checking the sharpness of its black blade, nearly letting her own blood in the process. Gripping the knife the way her father had taught her, she inched toward the closed driftwood door. Gathering herself once more, she pressed against it, first lightly and then with increasing force until the effort bordered on the kind which causes an expulsion of sound. There was something blocking the way. She pressed her face to the driftwood, but could only get a sliver of sight this way and no clue as to what was impeding her escape.

Trying to think of another way, she noticed that the chunk of soil that she'd torn from the frame had been replaced. It had been a rushed job, however, so she began pulling away at the soil until the chunk came away from the wall again in almost one solid piece.

She lowered her face to the hole and looked out. Turning her eyes as far downward as possible, she saw the wooden wedge that held the door in place from the outside. Quickly creating a new vision of terror and reprisal, one where her arm was staked to the door, she snaked her hand through the hole and reached for the wedge.

She realized her error in distance and withdrew her hand, then took the knife and plunged that through the door at the end of her arm. The tip of the knife found purchase in the wood, and after a strange and noisy coupling with the door, she managed to position herself with enough leverage to move the wooden wedge a short distance. She repeated this task three more times, lustily and with a growing anger, her confidence built up once again by lack of punishment. She was making noise now, she knew, but hoped it was not enough to carry on the wind and cause the man to come rushing back.

This thought thrust her into another sweaty appeal with the wooden block until finally it moved a substantial amount. She brought her arm back inside, and managed to push the door open enough that she thought she could squeeze out. It took longer than she had hoped, and about halfway through the process, with her clothes torn and her back soiled with black dirt, she wished she had tried to move the wedge a little further. But she pressed on, figuring forward was as good as backward at that point and eventually forged ahead out of the hovel and back into the afternoon sun.

Barely keeping her feet under her, Aida carried her momentum back toward the water's edge, and for the first time, it occurred to her how incomplete and risky her deception had been. Her father's boat was there, still sitting where she had left it. Surely, though it didn't seem to have been tampered with, it had been seen. When the moment of decision had come upon her, she had thought of hiding the boat as a good course of action, but now realized her error. Because of the boat, the man knew that someone was surely there. She froze in place, looking out over the water, realizing that the wedge in the door had not been placed to keep the door from blowing open, or whatever she'd hoped the man had thought, but rather to keep her inside. With a strange feeling blossoming in the back of her throat, she turned slowly back to the hovel.

And there he was, standing above the doorway, atop the hillock, watching her. One of her visions of consequence had been accurate. While she was fighting against the door, he had been there no distance away, waiting.

She moved slowly backward so as not to frighten him into action as if he were a wild animal. She crouched, eyes still on him, reaching for the oar she'd left on the beach.

He was motionless, watching.

He wore no leather above his waist, she saw, but had painted his chest in large swaths of red. He had no spear as she had envisioned, or any weapon at all. He was well coloured from the sun and his deep black hair was cut roughly at his shoulders. His beard was short and black, his eyes, though distant, seemed black as well. He held no menace in his stance, but instead seemed content in his observation.

Her hand found the oar; Aida turned and leapt into the boat, the force of her motion dislodging the craft from the beach. With one stoic push, she was free and clear, already hissing through the water.

She looked back only once when it occurred to her what had truly happened there at the end.

He had let her go.

*   *   *

He had let her go.

The thought would not leave her. It repeated in her mind the whole time she was waiting for their guard to slip, so she could get back to the boat. At first she assumed her excitement was fear, and she thought she'd avoided certain tragedy and death, never wishing to go back to that man again. The guarding of the boats was preposterous, she'd told them, for she had no desire to go back across the lake and be murdered.

But that's only what she thought she felt, what she was told she should feel. In actuality, she wanted to go back all along. She had misinterpreted her emotions. She was not afraid; she was wanting. Of what, she was not sure, be it knowledge or adventure, but she knew the wanting was everything. It was life, breath and everything worth being; no matter what her father or brothers said, she was going back at the first opportunity.

She ended up playing the good woman for nearly a month before their belief in her was solid and their trust returned. The morning after, she was in a boat, paddling through the fog once more.

Over the course of this second journey, she reflected on their reactions to her tale. They had known nothing, not one of them, of the other side of the lake. Sure, there were other men in the world; this was of no consequence. "Lucky she'd escaped" was the only insight they had, as if all men, inherently evil, existed to damage and destroy.

Not one of them, man, woman or child, was interested in who he was, or why he was there alone.

Except Aida. And though there'd been men aplenty since her transformation into womanhood, she'd found none of them desirable or interesting. Only this one, this stranger from another world held her interest. Over the month she'd been polite, but never let anyone within arm's length. The world she had known her whole life held no passion for her any longer.

When she arrived, he was there as if waiting.

He stood at the edge of the grass, shirtless and still, the same as when she had last laid eyes on him as if he were a dream revisited. When he saw her, he at first made no reaction, then slowly his hand rose to his chest. There, the only difference was the lack of red smeared across his torso, Aida noticed now. He turned and moved away quickly, soon disappearing into his hovel.

Now worried, Aida beached the boat. She had not known what to expect upon her return, but all her visions had been of confrontation, one sort or another. His departure, or a desire from him not to see her, had never entered her mind. The moments were long as she stood, watching the open door, awaiting his return.

When he reemerged, he was painted again; a smear of red, a hand's breadth wide from the middle of his abdomen to his armpit.

He returned to the spot at the edge of the grass and again stood still as if his departure had never occurred. There was a lightness in his eyes as if he wished to smile, but was unsure if that course of action was appropriate.

So Aida smiled first. His eyes alit even further, but still he kept his composure. They stood, only sand between them, for some time, before finally he broke their vigil by looking skyward. An expression of worry crept onto his face and he looked back at her, puzzled. She returned his look of puzzlement, to indicate she didn't know what he wanted. He held his hand up, a gesture to indicate that she wait where she was, and he turned and went back to the hillock.

During this new absence, it occurred to her that neither of them had yet tried to communicate verbally. Perhaps he was from a tribe that spoke a different language, but that did not seem to be the issue. It seemed rather as if their lack of vocalization was chosen by their hearts or minds. And they had stood, somehow comfortable, brimming with anticipation within that silence. It had been right, and she chose not to be the first to put an end to the pattern.

The man returned with a bow in hand, the other hand hidden at his back. A quiver, filled to brimming, was strapped to his hip. She thought she now understood his glance skyward. The day was moving along, and he wished to begin a hunt before twilight came.

Instinctively, they moved toward each other, stopping at the edge of the beach. Slowly, he brought his hand from behind his back. In his open palm lay the stone knife she had used to aid her escape during their first encounter. She looked at him, trying to interpret the gesture, and finally his smile could no longer be subdued. It broke across his face and transformed him into a spirited boy, light flickering at the corners of his eyes.

He gestured further, holding out the knife; understanding, she took it. Then, without warning, he turned and ran into the grass, heading westward with gleeful strides. She took after him, a laugh spilling from her lips as she ran.

They hunted that first day. He had set slips and traps in the woods, and she was given the rabbits to gut and carry, a skill her brothers had taught her while still young. They only once saw larger game. When he had set to loose an arrow, he stepped hard on a branch and scared the young doe away. She tried not to laugh. At first he looked hurt, then the boyish grin won out, splitting his face with the humor of the situation.

They brought three large hares back to the hillock near the beach and he carried wood, enough to start a fire with. They moved a short distance south along the beach, where he had built a fire pit and pulled some felled driftwood into a circle. There they sat, their silence carried from their initial face-off that morning, through the hunt, and into the evening. They needed no words as they ate, the man offering the most succulent pieces to Aida as he cooked them, and she taking some thankfully and politely refusing others. They ate well and were warm into the night.

It was very late and they both had taken turns falling asleep while sitting before the dying fire. The final time, he rose and stretched, his body making an involuntary noise. He stamped out the last embers of the fire and began walking away. Not knowing what else to do, Aida followed.

When they arrived at the hovel, he gestured for her to follow him inside. She hesitated and he noticed her trepidation. He smiled and showed her his palm, a gesture that was becoming familiar. It meant wait, be calm.

He disappeared into the darkness of the hovel where the moonlight wouldn't reach. Her eyes quickly adjusted to the darkness inside; she watched as he took something from his bed and returned to her at the doorway. He had removed the woven leather blanket from his corner nest and now spread it on the floor. He held his hand out, offering his bed with the matted grass and furs to her. When she still hesitated, he took the blanket at his feet and moved it further away from his bed. He looked up at her and smiled, as if he had made a fine joke. It alleviated the rest of her fears. She moved past him and into the hovel, settling down into the pile of furs.

To her surprise, he undressed before her, then stood naked for a long time. Again holding his hand up in a gesture of waiting, he moved toward her. She could hear her heart racing in her ears as she stared at his naked legs, the way the muscles roiled and tensed beneath the flesh. She felt heat well up in her stomach and begin to seep downward as he crouched before her, reaching out. Beside her, his hand found purchase and with a distinct motion, he plucked one of the furs from the bed. He rose, turned, and settled back down on his leather blanket, covering himself with the fur.

She felt the breath return to her and the heat in her stomach began to subside. But it did not go away altogether, and she wondered what that meant. Would she have wanted it, had he chosen to take her then and there? Was her fear once again simply excitement? These thoughts beckoned her into sleep and she dreamed womanly dreams throughout the night.

When she awoke, the door was open and the rising sun poured into the small space, filling it with joy. Her new friend was nowhere to be seen, but she thought she heard noise by the water.

She rose, wrapping a fur around her shoulders in case there was a morning chill, and stepped outside. He was there in the lake, still naked, standing with water just above his knees. He was splashing himself and taking small steps, adjusting to the temperature of the water. She approached, again finding herself staring at his legs, and the curve of his buttocks. This was the womanhood her elders had spoken of, this desire to have the touch of a man, to feel him all over. What she had not understood last night, this second viewing had clarified. She wanted this man.

He turned as if sensing her intent. When he saw her, he became embarrassed, but when he covered himself, he did not reach for his manhood, but rather his chest. He crossed both arms about his torso and lowered his head. She moved toward him, wishing to alleviate his shame, but he would not even look up. She noticed how the cold water of the lake had reduced his size, and felt the desire to see the situation remedied. And what better way to make him at ease than to show him her body in turn.

She dropped the fur at her feet and began to unlace her clothes. He looked up and catching her eyes, smiled sadly and shook his head. Still holding his arms in front of his chest, he left the water and without looking up at her, strode past and toward the hovel. She followed him inside, and found him opening a large wooden case, the edges of which were stained red. He turned to her as she entered; there was a soft anger in his eyes as if he wanted to be alone, but didn't have the heart to tell her so. She moved slowly, again, like that first meeting, treating him as if he were an animal so as not to frighten or surprise him.

She reached out, saw his arm tense, but continued, placing her fingers lightly upon him. With barely any pressure, she pressed his arm downward away from his chest. There, without the mask of dye, she saw what he seemed so ashamed of. There were three markings on his abdomen just below the bow of his chest as if an animal had clawed him, but they were very precise and deep, each mark equal in length and width. She raised her face to him, trying to create an affectionate but quizzical look. To her surprise, he was crying heavily, though some act of will kept his body still. Tears were pouring down his face and again, with no thought of her actions, she pressed her thumbs against them, blockading them, trying to dry them to no avail, but still trying. He gently grasped her wrists and took her hands away, then covered his face until he could staunch the flow of tears. Now she felt he wanted to be alone, so she left him and went outside to bathe in the sun and the lake, hoping to alleviate her worries.

Perhaps he had been watching from the hovel, for he did not emerge until she had dressed. The swath of red dye was again present, covering the markings. But now she knew they were there, and could see them beneath the dye. She moved to him and took his hand more forcefully than before, leading him back to the water's edge. There she cupped her hands in the water and splashed his chest. He took a step back, but she was not to be denied. She pressed on, splashing more water, then followed up by rubbing the dye with the tips of her fingers, cleaning it away from around the markings. He raised his arms as if about to grab her hand, then stopped himself with visible effort, swallowing hard and closing his eyes. It was clearly a great act of will that was allowing her to complete her efforts and she found herself becoming upset as well. Something was being cleansed here, beyond the obvious. She felt tears well up in her throat, but her defiant actions helped her focus and keep them at bay. When she was done cleaning the dye away, she looked him in the eyes, allowing him to see some of that defiance. His gaze had become gentle, his eyebrows raised and his brow unwrinkled. He briefly touched her forehead with his thumb.

They still did not speak though it only occurred to Aida at times of confusion which were few. For the most part, there was no need to clarify their feelings; they wore them for each other.

That evening, he again settled down onto his leather blanket, making no advances, allowing her the comfort of his bed. She felt the first seeds of doubt, that perhaps he did not want her in that way, or perhaps he couldn't perform the tasks of a man. She couldn't decide which situation would be worse.

She was awakened some time during the night by a sound that had seeped into her dreams. She opened her eyes and saw that the sobbing was coming from the real world. The man sat in the middle of the room, cross-legged, facing away from Aida. He was rocking rhythmically back and forth, accompanied by the low keening that had invaded her slumber. She crawled toward him and reached out, making brief contact with his naked back. He shuddered and squirmed away; a new sound, a rattling, escaped him.

Aida felt the need to speak for the first time, but instead touched him again. This time, as if registering what the contact was, his shuddering stopped. He swiveled on his buttocks, the source of the rattling sound revealing itself. In his hands, he held a necklace - a pale leather strap hung with teeth of different sizes and colors. Some were clearly animal teeth, for she had seen them in the death grins of various game throughout her life. She did not recognize others.

She caught his gaze and again saw the shame he had exhibited that morning. He held up the necklace, not as an offering, but as an admission. She reached her hand for it, but he snatched it away. Realizing he had startled her, he smiled strangely and raised his head to stare openly at the ceiling. It was a gesture she had seen before, one indicating that a person did not want to shed tears. As if to distract himself, he took the necklace and placed it over his head. It caught on his ears, causing the teeth to dangle before his wide eyes. He smiled and tilted his head, a new offering, one of humour to escape the uncomfortable situation. She forced a smile back. He shook his head, causing the teeth to clack together. They both smiled. He removed the necklace and sighed, whatever trauma he had experienced finally passing.

The emotions of the past few days, coupled with this strange outburst, gathered in Aida's chest, and her mind was swept away, all logical thought left by the wayside. She tugged at her laces with some strength, then forced her leathers over her head, exposing her naked breasts. She held the fur at her sides, creating an invitation for him to join her within.

This time, he did not hesitate. In moments he was upon her, forcing his mouth so hard onto hers that she could barely catch her breath. Before she could process the deep heat now rising from her middle and spreading through every limb, he had forced her leggings roughly down over her hips. She felt a moment of exposure before his probing tongue filled her mouth, taking all thoughts of her nakedness from her mind. She reached for him, her fingers brushing away the soil he had accumulated on his backside. His actions were not so caring and her earlier fear that he could not perform the sexual act was dashed aside by his abrupt and intense penetration. She felt the pressure and then a rush of pain and was momentarily shocked. She had been told it would hurt that first time, but she had not expected so much pain.

He was rough, taking her mouth hard in his, hand tangled in her hair. He moved her every way he wished, thrusting and wrenching. She thought the pain of his entry would subside, but his aggression kept the pain intense, and she began to wonder when the good feelings associated with the act would appear.

It was not, in its bare urgency, the way she had envisioned coupling with the man. He had seemed simple and gentle, but there was clearly a beast beneath that shell. Again, without word or thought, only instinct, her body responded. She began to press against him with her hands, wanting to alleviate at least the weight of his presence. He responded, by forcing her down, harder, and further, pulling her hair until she faced the wall at her back. A noise began to come from her throat, not speech, but a low squeal of displeasure and she began to hit his back with her palms. He again responded, the noise clearly unsettling him, and placed his forearm on her throat.

The pain there instantly made her forget the pain of her deflowering as she felt the tissues of her throat grind painfully together. She tried to gasp, but could bring in no air. With all her strength, she forced her head forward, trying to catch his eyes with hers. She wanted to somehow let him know he was hurting her badly, but he wasn't watching her.

He was looking down, almost averting his gaze, as tears fell freely from his eyes. Feeling her eyes upon him, he pressed down harder with his forearm and the sobbing which had begun the whole incident started anew.

And at that last moment, she understood why he was alone. He had no desire to kill her; he was simpler than that. He shed tears for this was his way, to maim and destroy, and he could not help himself. His open gaze flashed before her mind's eye, the way he smiled, the way they needn't speak because he was transparent in his emotion. Like a child.

Deep down, a part of her was telling her to fight, but it was an easy voice to ignore. It had, after all, been her own mistake; and these were the consequences of womanhood. At the end, she smelled rain, and remembered it fondly, the purity of it.

*   *   *

He took her in the boat, his chest freshly dyed, to cover the manmade markings of his shame. The fog cleared as he approached the other side of the lake. There were few people by the water, mostly children. They gathered as he brought the boat up onto the sand, then quickly dispersed when they saw his cargo.

He carried the girl, limp and beautiful, to the center of the village.

There he knelt, waiting for the men folk, the elders to see. Slowly they did, but he barely heard their shocked reactions and their mournful wails. He had heard the like before, and felt numb to their effects. He had gone beyond them, and was here now to admit his crime and face his consequences.

After a long time, only the warriors remained - grandfathers, fathers and brothers. They encircled him and watched him carefully. A man, perhaps the father, approached and retrieved the body.

He waited for the father's departure before looking up, finally meeting the eyes of those gathered. Here, he had laid himself at their feet and now he prayed for the mercy his own tribe had not given him. He found hope in those eyes, for they seemed composed, these warriors.

A cry erupted from somewhere and his heart sank. He was a monster, and monsters do as monsters do. He couldn't help it.

He had taken the teeth.

The father returned, a flame in his eyes, but he spoke with composure. Their eyes were cold when they began and they beat him heartily until death.

Untitled

David Hunter

The Disappearing Act

Andrea Beça

The roses didn't taste that bad at first, despite the fact that they were at least a week old. They had kept well, and had a faint perfume flavour to them during the first few chews. Once she reached the centre, however, where all of the flower's reproductive organs are housed, the rose became almost unbearably tart. Mind you, she wasn't certain that this was due to the stamen, or whatever it was called, but she thought if anything, it would have been that. The reproductive organs, that is. Lucy would have known what they were called; she always had her face buried in her books. You would have thought she was hiding herself away the way she stayed in her room absorbing all that knowledge at such a ridiculous rate. She got it from Douglas, of course. All of the good traits came from him. 'Daddy knows best' and all that. Pondering this, Laurie continued to chew, her right eye welling with tears in response to the bitterness of the bouquet, until all twelve of the roses were gone. The thorns, although somewhat more challenging, did not faze her; by this point, the taste of blood had grown somewhat comforting.

It took her a week to even enter the room. She spent the first six days walking past the closed door on her tiptoes, pretending Lucy was asleep on the other side. On the seventh day, she approached the door and knocked quietly. When there was no answer, she knocked again, a little louder. "Lucy," she whispered. No answer. "I'm coming in," she threatened with a playful giggle, the way she had often done when Lucy was just a little girl.

There was only one box left behind, stuck in the corner of the room and labelled *books to give away* in Lucy's writing. Laurie sat in the middle of the room and pulled the box toward her. A glint of light caught the corner of her eye: Lucy's locket. It must have fallen off while she was packing, staying stuck under the one box she hadn't even taken with her. Laurie let the delicate gold chain fall between her fingers, the small heart cold in the palm of her hand. She used her thumbnail to open it. On one side, Douglas at age twenty or so: handsome, hopeful, smiling. One the other, Laurie's own face reflected back at her, with a much more youthful glow. Not much older, in fact, than Lucy was now.

Before she could reason with herself, she dangled the chain above her face, letting the heart fall onto her tongue. Before she could reason with herself any further, the rest of the chain fell in and Laurie swallowed hard; she felt somewhat satisfied. Before another week had passed, most of the books were gone, too. Laurie found that if she took a sip of red wine along with a shred of paper and held both in her mouth for a period of time, an easy-to-swallow pulp would form. She recycled the covers – she was new at this yet.

Douglas came over once. Of course, he had kept his keys. Laurie had not even considered this possibility; it had been his choice to leave. He waltzed into the kitchen without so much as knocking. She was sitting at the dining table in her robe and slippers, her hands wrapped around a mug of hot water with lemon.

"What's happened to you?"

"When did you get here?"

"What's happened to your face, Laurie?"

"Why didn't you even knock?"

"What is this? Scrabble? You're in your pyjamas at four in the afternoon, Laurie. Your mouth is covered in sores. And you're playing Scrabble by yourself. Should I be worrying about you?"

"They're not sores, Douglas. They're cuts. You make me sound diseased. I'm not diseased, Douglas. I'm not a disease."

"Jesus Christ!" Douglas stormed out of the room, "Fucking typical!"

While he was away, Laurie swallowed an 'A', two 'I's, and the only 'Q' in the game. She listened to him rifling through her personal belongings in their old bedroom and swallowed a 'D', 'O', 'U'. She was fishing through the bag for a 'G' when he returned, exasperated.

"Have you seen Lucy's locket?"

"No."

"Are you sure, Laurie?"

"Stop speaking to me like a child, Douglas. I said I haven't seen it."

"What about the box of books she left in her room?"

"What about it?"

"Maybe it fell into the box."

"There was no box."

"What are you talking about?"

"I said there was no box."

Douglas looked at Laurie the way he had been trained to look at everyone in his life: the way doctors look at their patients. After a brief moment, he turned, and without a single word, slammed the front door behind him. Laurie reached into the pocket of her robe, producing a small light bulb. She wrapped it in the tea towel that normally hung over the handle of the oven and then retrieved her hammer from the junk drawer. Once it was broken into more manageable pieces, Laurie got to work on the light bulb and forgot all about Douglas.

She would have forgotten the exchange had Douglas not sent one of his colleagues over to see her a few days later. By that time there were only two 'T's and a 'B' left over. Laurie peered out into the world through a crack in the curtains which always remained closed over her front window. She recognized him from the hospital, though he worked on a different floor than Douglas, in the psychiatry ward. Although he rang the bell numerous times, she did not go to the door. Instead, she rummaged through her junk drawer for her fabric scissors and started from the bottom up. She didn't do all the curtains, but rather skimmed off the lower edge. After all, privacy was still a concern.

Laurie did not have many regrets in her life. Even getting pregnant at seventeen was better than many had told her it would be; in the end, she got a baby out of it. And in her fifteen years of life, Lucy had outshone all the pain and struggle, all the arguments over 'this sham of a marriage.' What Laurie regretted was not realizing that the sham was holding things together.

She would have regretted not cluing in and swallowing her divorce forms only months earlier, but was too busy tearing the engagement announcement for Douglas and *her* into tiny pieces. She liked the feeling of the newsprint dissolving against the roof of her mouth before she washed it down with boiling hot coffee.

She was sitting in the attic, swallowing the flower-shaped buttons off one of Lucy's baby dresses when the pains started. She crunched herself into a foetal position and continued to pick the pink daisies off, one by one. When she started to cough blood into the soft pink satin dress, Laurie produced her trusty pair of scissors from her pocket and worked it down in small patches. It was ruined now, anyway. When she was finished, she used the point of the scissors to dial 911 – she had swallowed all of the buttons off her cordless handset days before.

As it turned out, it was not the light bulbs causing the problems as Laurie had assumed. Only when the doctors told her that it was the full ball of purple knitting yarn that she had ingested did she remember that her grandmother's cat had died from that very symptom. She was hooked up to an IV and told that the doctors would need to wait to see if she could pass the doorknobs from the kitchen cupboards naturally. They were tangled in the yarn along with 18 household screws and bolts and a few of the Scrabble tiles. The morphine eased the pain, but she could still feel the pressure, the intense pressure in her abdomen, pressing against her organs, making it difficult for her to breathe. In some ways, it reminded her of being pregnant with Lucy. Her daughter had always been a kicker.

They sent her a dozen red roses a few days into her stay. She wasn't sure whose idea it was to send red roses – romantic flowers – of all the flowers, especially since the accompanying card was clearly written by *her*:

For Laurie,

We all hope you are feeling well soon!

With Love, Douglas, Lucy, and Sherry

(P.S. We thought it would be best to keep Lucy from seeing you in the hospital. We're sure you understand!)

For the first couple of days, she was too weak to do anything but think about it. This gave her a great deal of time to fixate upon the 'we's' with which the note had been littered. After a while, she picked her wedding band off the side table, looping it around the very tip of her tongue, pressing it against the inside of her cheek, making imprints on her lips with it. Laurie swallowed it with the orange juice they made her drink every morning, and then slowly worked down the note over a course of 48 hours. On day nine, they were forced to up her dosage of painkillers. She refused to sign the surgery waiver, insisting on waiting just a few more days. It was then that she got to work on the roses.

In Fields of Butterfly Flames

Steve Wade

A St. Bernard pup, my instant pal, he bounded straight to me from the litter of four and the mama dog when I went to collect him, hardly weaned that evening. I brought him home; he didn't last long. Two days later, I came in from working the fields to find his little bedraggled body floating in the rusty barrel drum. On the ground beside the barrel lay a garden rake with congealed blood and white dog hairs clinging to its steel teeth.

The instant thrumming that started up in my head gave way to petrified anger as I pressed his sopping, lifeless carcass to my face. The heightened doggy smell pervaded my senses and the freezing wetness soaked through my overalls, chilling me. There I knelt, shivering and sniveling next to the unused outhouse until the September evening closed, my little pal's remains in my arms, the uneven, stony earth biting into my knees.

The moon threw a bony light across the land. The same ghostly luminosity that had played with the elongated shadows a year before. That terrible night Dale never came home. In the pre-dawn light, I found him - what was left of our second born - our only surviving son.

Numbed and helpless, I pushed to my feet and headed for the house; in my arms was the St Bernard puppy I hadn't yet named.

Shona was where I knew she'd be - at the kitchen table. Spread before her like tarot cards were family photos taken from the albums featuring Dale, many of them with sides sheared into curved contours where she'd long ago cut out the images of Robert, our eldest, canceling him as though he had never been. As if by denying Robert's life, she could erase what he'd done to our family and our family home.

In the photos, Dale as an infant; Dale's first steps; Dale, red-faced, pedaling a tricycle on his third birthday; Dale sitting atop the grey Shetland colt; Dale at the seaside; his first communion, his confirmation; Dale, through a smile that wasn't a smile, blowing out eighteen candles on a birthday cake; his nineteenth and twentieth birthdays. And in Shona's hand, as usual, the photo of a cake featuring a Batman motif and the number twenty-one – the birthday Shona had insisted we celebrate in Dale's absence.

With the dead pup cradled in my arms, I waited for Shona to release the photo her thumbs caressed. She didn't. I clenched my eyes tight and shook my head in a futile effort to get rid of the image that wouldn't leave me alone: Shona bundling the St. Bernard pup into the barrel. Her maddened, contorted features as she used the garden rake to batter and plunge the screaming, terrified animal beneath the drowning waters.

With bile rising into my throat, I turned from her and went to the living room.

There I placed the pup's body on the rug in front of the hearth, scrunched up some old newspapers and got a fire going to dry out his coat before burial in the morning.

Over the next few weeks, I avoided Shona for the most part. Did only the necessary jobs to be done with the cattle in the fields and the milking station; freeing me with the time I needed to devote to a special project.

The evening I'd been working towards arrived. Only a month since the pup's drowning, and not fully a year since Dale went away, my gut told me Shona still needed much more time. I guessed it'd be this way. That's why I'd spent the last few weeks getting the outhouse ready for the new arrival: put in aluminum window frames with dark, frosted glass and inside shutters, took care of all those areas where draughts might sneak in, and got hold of a big wicker basket with blankets where he could sleep.

I re-plastered the inside walls, put in a toilet and sink, rewired the electricity, warmed the drying plaster with a small heater and stuck in a small cooker and mini fridge. The old sofa I'd kept stored in the barn would do me.

The renovated outhouse would also give me a place to escape from Shona; lately, she'd been depressing me like I never thought possible. Far more cosy in the house, my new pal and me would do fine out there. As for Shona mooching around the outhouse, I wasn't concerned. She seldom left the house anymore.

Because my new pal would be quite young, my plan was to stay with him nights, right up until I felt Shona was ready to accept him in the house. No way I would have left him on his own on that cold stone floor beneath those rafters. Not at night time.

Shona wouldn't be bothered by my absence. The truth is that we hadn't slept in the same bed these past months.

Anyway, I could hardly contain my excitement that first evening. He was finally safe there in his basket where I had left him. Just how I imagined it. I'd picked him up early that morning. Drove over a hundred miles to get him. He wailed and whimpered for hours for his mama. That was the toughest part of it. He refused to take food and drink; his eyes retreated from mine whenever I got too close, and his body froze like a lamb with hypothermia.

I left a bowl of milk near his basket, and in another bowl, some of the reheated rabbit stew I'd cooked specially up the night before. He'd come round. As I said, he was young.

I was right. However, I'd been starting to doubt my convictions after three or four days. I came very close to bundling him back into the Pajero, driving back to where I picked him up and depositing him in the street. But one day when I came in from the fields at lunchtime, he toppled out of his basket and padded right up to me.

"Hey," I said. "Hello. There's a good boy. You ready to be my friend now?"

He nodded up at me, a tiny, even-toothed smile on his face. "Yeah," he said and jerked up his arms, like a game he was maybe used to playing. "Yeah," he repeated.

"Okay," I said, and playfully copied his arm movements. I then ruffled his curly head, his hair the same russet as Dale's, except his had been straight. One of the reasons I'd chosen him: his hair.

Just like the boys when they were kids, my little pal was temperamental. One moment, he was giggling and turning the potato chips on his plate into impromptu vehicles and making engine noises, the next he was blubbering for his mama again. But as soon as I told him we were going to drive the tractor around the fields, he forgot all about his mama. He even put on some of the clothes I'd left out for him. Dale's clothes: striped trousers, a Batman T-shirt, and a pair of blue wellies, stuff that Shona'd kept for a million years. She's a hoarder, Shona. Holds onto everything.

Sitting upfront in the tractor cabin, he could have been one of the boys. He pointed at the screaming seagulls the way the boys used to, and giggled at the blades churning up the earth; his hair smelt just the way theirs did, of shampoo and vitality.

The only time he got a bit confused was when I called him 'Dale'. He stuck out his lower lip, cried and told me his real name. I eased down on the brakes, killed the engine, and explained that we were playing a pretend game. He could make believe I was his daddy, couldn't he? And I could pretend his name was Dale.

"You're not my daddy," he said, his back pressed to the tractor door, his features a knot of confusion and fear, the way he appeared the day he arrived.

"No, of course I'm not." I ruffled his untidy hair. "How about 'Pa'? Why don't you call me Pa?"

He made no answer, but his crying stopped. He twisted round, his face and palms pressed against the glass.

"Look," he said, pointing at the darkening sky. "A nail."

Puzzled at first by what he meant, I got it when he glanced and giggled at his own wiggling thumb. A fingernail. He saw the quarter moon set in the charcoal blue sky as a fingernail clipping. What a clever kid. He and Dale really might have been the same boy. Despite being two years younger, Dale was much smarter than Robert. Always was.

For my little pal and me, the following weeks fell into a routine that I wished could've lasted forever. Once I'd milked the cattle, put them out to graze in the low fields, weather permitting, and fed and watered the bay mare, I'd return to Dale – the newest Dale. He'd already be up, sleepy-eyed and waiting. I'd prepare his Coco Pops and juice, get him cleaned up, and then out to the fields. There the two of us would talk, laugh and sing our way through the morning and into the evening in the tractor cabin or mucking about in the fields.

Soon with the limited daylight and Hallowe'en drawing near, there was less reason for us to be in the fields, the crops on a go-slow. Just as well. I was worried about the effect that the drop in temperature might have on the lad. This concern turned into an obsession. The old two-bar electric heater and small blow heater hardly made a difference in our converted outhouse, so I pulled out a long forgotten baseboard heater from a load of junk in the cowshed.

But despite the three heaters being turned up full, the place never reached room temperature. Must have been the stone floor and the original dampness. So when little Dale began coughing this nasty cough that sounded like he might tear his throat; I knew the time had come. Time to introduce him to Shona.

Completely hidden by the band of conifers, I could make out Shona's familiar seated figure in the square of light at the kitchen table when I emerged along the dirt path, clutching Dale's hand. Not knowing for sure how Shona might react when she saw the boy, I warned him that the lady we were going to visit wasn't well. She cried a lot, I told him. Sometimes she screamed. And her eyes were big, like an owl's eyes. But there was no need for him to be afraid. After all, I was with him. I'd never let anything happen to him. His pa would protect him.

"Shona," I said after wiping my feet across the worn straw doormat. "I've got a surprise for you."

Just as I'd foreseen, Shona initially ignored me. Her maddened eyes kept right on scouring the photos before her as if she might yet detect the missing minutiae to undo the unanswerable.

"Son," I said, directing the boy in front of me by the shoulders. "This is your ... this is Shona."

In my palms, I felt his resistance like the first strike of a brown trout. That sense of being hyper-connected to another living creature, its pulse firing along the fishing line and coursing through you, so you and it are indistinguishable: two beings, one soul.

I smiled reassuringly down at his upturned face, his mouth shaping the word 'Pa' – I was almost sure of it.

The terrible sound that peeled from Shona then was the scream I'd last heard the morning I came through the open kitchen door, Dale's lifeless body draped across my shoulders in a fireman's lift, branded around his neck the hanging mark left by the blue rope that I sometimes used as a makeshift halter for the bay mare.

"You're frightening him, Shona. Please."

Shaking her head, she stood wedged between the counter and the accidentally overturned kitchen table, her swollen eyes predatory like a cornered beast.

Dale had turned away from her, his whole face clenched, his arms about my leg. I picked him up.

"Pa," he said. "Pa."

About to escape clutching the boy, Shona's frozen face shifted, her attention on the scattered photos lying on the black and white tiled floor. A new terror played in her features. And then she was on her knees, scratching at the photos' corners, gathering them together. But what happened next, I could never have foreseen.

Dale indicated he wanted to be put down. He then tottered to Shona, crouched next to her and began to scoop up some of the photos. Shona jerked away from him, her head sideways, her eyes jammed in their corners.

My entire being coiled, primed to intervene as I watched Shona's eyes, bubbles in a spirit level, right themselves slowly as she twisted her face towards Dale. The smile curled her lips, retransforming, returning to the once beautiful face that, till then, taunted me like a memory of something that never was.

"Who's this?" she asked, her gaze locked on Dale the way a lioness locks onto a grazing gazelle from behind tall grass. "Where did you get him?"

"He needs us to look after him," I said. Too soon to even consider using his name in front of Shona. Later. That would come later.

"He's beautiful," she said.

On her knees she opened her arms. Dale hesitated. Twisted round to me. Sweating, I nodded. And as in a rare vignette, one that doesn't terrify, dreamed under heavy fever, it happened. Dale stumbled forward and fell into Shona's motherly embrace.

"There, there," she said. "*Mo chuisle. Mo chuisle mo chroi*," using the language of her rural background. My pulse. Pulse of my heart.

From that moment, Shona and Dale were as inseparable and steadfast as a successful peach and pear tree grafting.

Through the kitchen windows, shafts of autumn sunlight animated their lively togetherness in the mornings. Dale sang nursery rhymes with Shona, his piping voice blending with the warbling and trilling that poured in from the hazel trees and yew hedging in the garden. Evening times, they sat together at the kitchen table, making fairy cakes and gingerbread men. From a book I hadn't seen for years, Shona read him tales of ants, eagles, wolves, lions, foxes and crows. Dale's eyes swelled bigger than a puppy's, his laughing voice pre-empting words spoken by fabled creatures whose lives he already knew and relived during Shona's reading.

All seemed renewed. Like the imminent catastrophes magically overridden in those fantastic fables, beauty and harmony had been restored to the world. Yet inside my stomach, there bubbled something evil, a warning that wouldn't leave me alone. And I, in turn, refused the temptation to leave Dale alone with Shona. Perhaps because she insisted Dale call her by her name. While she only ever addressed Dale as 'love' or '*a stor mo chroi*' – darling of my heart.

Could it be that I imagined it? But there was another thing: an occasional glint in Shona's eyes reminded me of certain dogs I'd owned or encountered over the years. A wild look, an emptiness that cancelled every trace of thousands of years' domesticity would sizzle in their canine eyes. The glint in her eyes flashed before the attack, the sudden, unexpected snap and snarl when teeth connected with outstretched hand.

Never would I allow her to be alone with him, I vowed. Not ever.

In the early mornings, I tried to ignore the dairy herd lowing in the barn. Not until Dale was up and finished his breakfast did I leave the house with him in my arms or tottering sleepily beside me. I'd removed the big basket from the outhouse and placed it in the milking station. While I got the milking machine going and hooked up the teat cups, Dale curled up under his blankets, asked endless questions, sang snatches of nursery rhymes and usually fell asleep.

It was Shona's endless pleading that altered this routine.

"A little mite," she kept at me. "And you dragging him out into the cold. Is it mad you are?"

"Good for the lad," I said. "It'll toughen him up. Turn him into a hardy soul."

But Shona wouldn't leave off her badgering. And she seemed to be deteriorating again. The signs were obvious. Even pulled out the photo album one afternoon.

Finally I relented. No choice. But not before I'd re-explained to Dale that Shona wasn't well, that sometimes adults who are unwell do things they don't mean to, like hurt people. I gave him a spare key to the outhouse, showed him how to use it and lock himself inside should he ever feel that Shona was going to hurt him. He was to stay there till I came to get him.

"Do you understand? You come here, lock yourself in like this and I'll be here soon, okay?"

He got it. I could tell. Such a bright kid.

Unconvinced about Shona's mental state, I hurried in from the milking station with beating temples and knotted stomach at what horror scene awaited me that first day I left him alone with her. I continued this pattern at half-hour intervals throughout the week. During that period, I could hardly look at my dinner.

But just when the beating in my head began to ease, and a healthy appetite usurped my twisted stomach, I emerged from the conifer grove one evening to a sight that caught me in the solar plexus. Hot, bitter bile erupted from my throat and spilled through my lips. Enervated, I drew my sleeve across my mouth and squinted towards the house.

In the kitchen window, a shimmering orange light that centered on the ledge replaced the normal light: the pumpkin they'd been carving that afternoon. Absent were Dale and Shona's figures.

I broke into an impulsive sprint and reached the house in seconds.

"Dale," I shouted as I pounded through the house. "Shona! Dale!" I heard my detached voice bellowing while I pulled open doors, crashed into furniture and fittings and tore away crumpled bedclothes.

Gone - both of them. What had she done? What had I let that fiend do?

In my urgency to get back down the stairs, I slipped. Something detonated inside my ankle, sending a metallic sheet of pain exploding across my vision. Working my way back onto my feet at the bottom of the stairs, a follow-up explosion, raw and crimson, erupted behind my eyes, buckling me like a shot deer. Pushing through the blinding pain, I dragged myself over the floor to the kitchen. There I summoned willpower and strength greater than I could have imagined I possessed, and pressed, pulled and pushed my way on one leg.

Using the sweeping brush as a crutch, I tried to steel myself against the inevitable horror forming in my head. The barrel drum. I had to get to the barrel drum.

Every movement down the three steps from the kitchen into the yard brought intolerable sledgehammer blows slamming against my ankle. I clenched my teeth and released intermittent growls: ugly, guttural sounds, the snarls of a creature in deep distress, or a murderer, maybe, wedded to the moment when his blade sears flesh, blood splashes and gushes hotly, soaking his killing hands and soul with satiated lust and love.

Too far from the shimmering light in the kitchen window, I could just about make out the palette that acted as a makeshift lid removed and resting against the barrel's side.

Fractured images of the drowned pup, of Dale's stiffened body hanging from the outhouse rafters and of Robert, almost two years before him on the floor of that same outhouse, his head half-blown away, my Magnum hunting rifle next to him, bleeding his life away in my lap. The images splashed about among the swirling pain.

The barrel, half-hidden by the shade thrown beneath the eaves of the low-pitched roof made it impossible to see inside the container. I plunged my arm through the blackened water up to my shoulder. The Arctic coldness cut into my flesh, right through to the bone marrow, gave instant respite from the intolerable burning that flailed my ankle.

Empty. The barrel was empty.

Relieved, confused and terrified, I snapped my head backwards at the night sky and cursed the nothingness. I welcomed the sickening pain shooting from my ankle to my head.

Robert and Dale dead. As their father, their deaths somehow belonged to me. Now I had surely killed Dale again.

More than pain, I too deserved death. But before I accepted and administered the self-inflicted punishment, I had to behold Dale's slain, twisted form. My instincts pushed me on through the yard towards the outhouse.

Unaccustomed to strange movements at night, the cattle hoofed about uneasily in the barn, grunting and complaining. From her stable, the bay mare whinnied and blew for my attention. I limped onward towards the outhouse.

Drawing near, I thought I could see a sliver of light slicing through the window shutter. I pushed on harder.

I reached the door and scrabbled in my overalls for the keys; I could swear I heard a voice or voices whispering inside. I stopped. I listened. ... Yes. Shona's voice. Jesus, it couldn't be ... , could it? I eased down the door handle and peered through the gap.

Silence now. Then from behind the door ...

"Boo!" Dale.

I fell backwards, renewed pain lacerating my ankle. But I didn't care.

"Dale," I said. "Dale. You're ... You're okay!"

"Pa fall down, Shona," he said twisting round to her. "Pa fall down." He came to me, his little hands gripping my arm, his face fully concerned in a huge effort to drag me to my feet.

"Oh my God," Shona said, stepping into the night. "Are you okay?"

I countered Shona's immediate suggestion that she call an ambulance.

"No, Shona. "I'll be fine. Really. It's just a sprain. Ice. You guys help me inside and, eh, ice. From the mini fridge. Ice." Ensuring Shona was fully focused my way, I allowed my eyes to jump in Dale's direction. I raised my eyebrows and nodded. A look I hope she'd get.

Alighting on Dale, her eyes narrowed. She pursed her lips. She got it. Neither one of us needed the authorities sniffing around the farm.

They helped me inside. Then Shona made up an ice-pack, placed a mug of tea before me and explained how Dale had brought her by the hand to 'the uddy house.' She and Dale sat down together at the table and got on with what they'd clearly been doing before I arrived.

"Look," she said to Dale. "I found another one that fits."

Dale clapped his hands and giggled.

Sticking the cut up photos back together. Christ. She'd kept the images of Robert. She never could discard anything.

"Oh, look," she said. "There you are with Robert, Dale. The day we had the picnic by the lake. The day it snowed in March."

Another explosion rocketed skyward in my head. But this time, a fireworks explosion crowded with an unbearable feeling of pure joy. But as the coloured trails and sparks burned away, they took with them my fleeting elation. Deposited in its place despair – instant, utter and complete.

Robert. Robert and Dale. Dale and Robert. Never were two lads more inseparable than our boys. Two years between them, they were best buddies from the day we brought Dale home from the hospital. So close were they that Dale stuck right by his big brother when Robert got sick, when Robert's head betrayed him, made him think crazy thoughts and do terrible things.

Like that summer, Robert's last summer, he trapped butterflies. Convinced the butterfly swarms were descending on the farm as a locust plague. He started out by pinning the insects to the old picnic table by the lake with bramble bush thorns. He'd then place a magnifying glass between them and the sun, his eyes widening and his nostrils expanding as he pulled in the wispy smoke plumes rising from the smouldering carcasses.

A failure on my part to get the boy help, I admit it. He graduated to trapping butterflies in the hundreds. That's all he did that summer. Trapped them and kept them in an old reptile cage he had in his bedroom. Sometimes he'd set them free in the room and just sit in his computer chair, this look on his face, watching the butterflies flit about, alighting on bookshelves and picture-frames, or thrashing against the window.

I was afraid of the consequences, Shona too. We discussed it. We'd work through his troubles as a family.

Too late. I got a call one afternoon from the emergency services to get back quickly to the farm. Shona, Dale and I were operating the vegetable stall at the weekend market. There'd been an accident, the guy on the phone warned.

The flames were still devouring the farmhouse when I pulled up outside the gate to our home: patrol cars, fire brigades and flashing lights. the police or the firemen had cordoned off the entrance. Neighbours had gathered.

"Robert," I shouted at the policemen trying to restrain me from pushing past the bodies and the vehicles. "My son Robert is inside. Please, I have to …"

"He's safe," the sergeant said, his hands on my shoulders. "We have him. He's safe. It's okay." For his own safety, he told me, they had him in one of the cars. He pointed.

I pushed past.

"Excuse me," I said. "My son. Can you let me through, please?" The crowd gave way.

"Robert," I said, tugging open the car door. "Robert, are you okay? What happened?"

But Robert was already somewhere else. Wasn't even aware of my presence. His bloated face, crammed with concentration, never shifted from the inferno, the flames flickering in his pupils and dancing on his skin. From his throat, a sickening, high-pitched keening caused the guard seated next to him to snap the cuffs attached to their wrists.

"Relax," the young guard said. "Take it easy now."

I frowned at the handcuffs and then at the guard.

"For his own safety," the guard said. "For his safety, sir."

For Robert's safety and ours, we finally had him committed for a while, but he talked us into getting the doctor to sign his release, the provision being that he continue to take the prescribed drugs.

Robert fooled us there too.

Twenty-three months. Dale waited twenty-three months before he followed Robert. We failed to read the signs. All summer, he'd been talking about how, on his next birthday, he'd be exactly the age Robert was when he went away. Dale just couldn't cope without him.

Tomorrow was going to be Halloween. I'd get Shona to drive into town for a Batman outfit. Then, in the evening, we could all head off like a family in Shona's car to some other town - a far away town, where nobody knew us. Shona would understand. Crowded with compassion now, she was ready to forgive. While I sat in the car with my bandaged ankle, she and Dale could go 'trick or treating'. The perfect day and time to seek out Dale's big brother Robert, lost and lonely out there somewhere, waiting. Waiting for forgiveness.

With Child

Katie Monahan

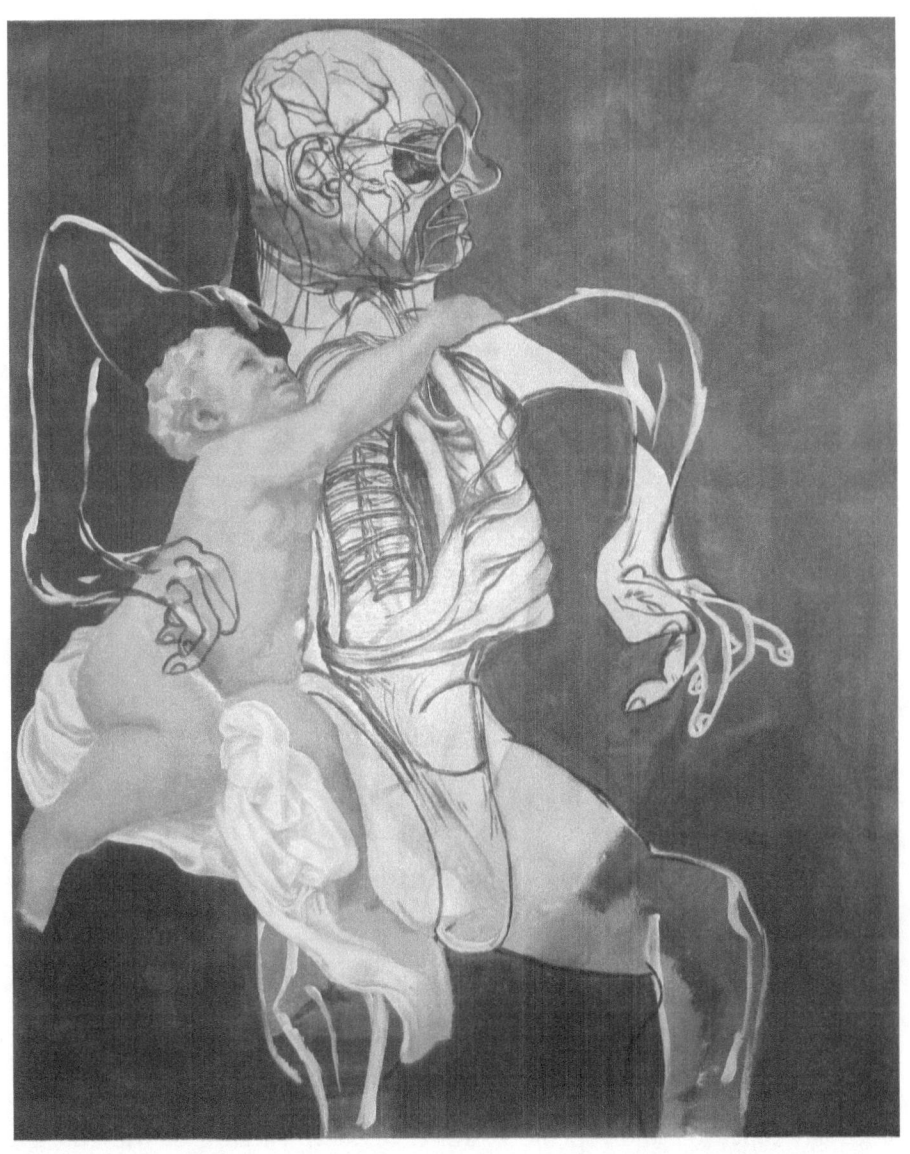

The Wife of Moby Dick

John Brooke

In August, when the humidex entered the oppressive zone, the girls gave in to pain and anger. They said, "Drastic moods for drastic measures!" - which was not quite how we had heard it. Still, their logic wasn't wrong.

That day, Aimée came up the alley lugging groceries, ranting at her son. "I don't like you much right now, *jeune homme*! I *said*, you are pissing me off, Lambert!" The boy was skipping around and around his suffering ma. It looked like a hopscotch pattern - *one foot, one foot, two foot, one*...repeated and repeated, empty headed, careless of the ghastly weather. "*Calisse*! can't you give *maman* a break!" Voila: Aimée's migraine, Montreal heat.

We were thinking Lambert's not mean, he's only seven - when Chimmy's prayer cut through from above.

Milli came out and slammed the door and started hanging washing. At every move of Milli's line, the rusty spool screeched hard. The sound was torturous, worse than the proverbial fingers across a blackboard; it was a scream from marriage hell.

Between each bitter yank, Chimmy's prayer leaked free. "*Bon,*" we said, "*la guerre continue.*" When Chim went to China seeking business opportunities he did not come home for a year. When he finally shows up he's empty handed, nothing for his Milli but this useless prayer. Chim's anguished chant carried loud and strangely from the murky gloom behind their kitchen door. The knife-sharp rip of a rusty spool was Milli's only weapon. When Chimmy prayed, Milli came out and worked the line. She always seemed to have fresh washing, and that day it got to Brigitte's heart.

Brigitte was on her step, moping, when she burst out sobbing. She was struggling with a loss of purpose. No man, no job. Keeping her child clean justified Brigitte's empty life; the endless noise of her washing machine was Brigitte's way of proving she was a useful mom. We lived with it. Until this summer, when Brigitte's feckless ex somehow found some cash and paid to send the kid to camp, leaving Brigitte with no excuse to do her Sunshine's clothes three times a day. It was coming on a month. That day, the sight of Milli hanging washing made something crack and out it poured, all that wasted love.

When Brigitte lost it, her dog Marco began to yap something horrible, while Aimée cursed like a cheated whore, "Damn you! Curse you, rude unholy boy!" and the methodic piercing scrape of Milli's line pushed back and back at Chimmy's bizarre prayer.

We sat and watched it, a small circus of misery gathering under the dog-day sky, the innocent clown Lambert, skipping in circles, counting it down in the sweetest voice, "*Skyblue, nine, seven, eight, six, four,*" incessant, tuneless, mindless, over and over and over again.

Fausto was on his porch in his chair like always, sheltering behind a rim of shade, talking on his cell. He had a bike scam going strong since May. The junkies would steal a bike and bring it to the alley. Fausto would give them cash and make a call. That woman he hired to shop and clean after Angelina died had a van. She'd arrive, pay Fausto, and take it off his hands. He had an almost-new 16-speed to unload that day. We watched as Fausto frowned and gestured. Maybe they were talking price.

When Aimée took a nasty swipe at young Lambert, he ducked and skipped onto Fausto's yard, chanting sweet and high, "*Eight you live, Nine you die, Ten you eat a bogey pie!*" His mother stood at the edge of Fausto's paving, beside herself with fury, berating, threatening and accusing. "You're an unruly little bastard! I will! ...I'll send you away!"

Brigitte was not a big woman: that's why she had the dog. She had a desperate stranglehold on Marco's leash as he dragged her around the fence and onto Fausto's yard, distraught, tears cascading, gazing up at bitter Milli hanging laundry with a vengeance as Chim's prayer ebbed and flowed in the commotion. And though Brigitte's blubbering was truly morbid, the sadder thing was Marco. He was snapping, wild to climb the stairs and get his nose in Milli's basket. Brigitte's maternal obsession had gotten deeply under Marco's canine skin – poor beast, barking like a shattered addict at the scent of cool wet things! While Lambert skipped and Aimee screamed like a horrid thing from hell.

Normally Fausto would shrug, "Not my kid, not my dog, not my problem." That day, with a deal on the line, the ugly heat and confounding noise put Fausto on defense. He turned away, phone tight to one ear, hand cupped tight to the other, shouted, "Say again!"

Dregs of Milli's wash water dripped through the grate and fell on Fausto's head. We watched Fausto squinting upward into the soles of Milli's shifting slippers. She wouldn't stop, pegging, pegging, now sending Chimmy's giant jockey shorts screeching across the sky.

We saw Fausto lose his thread. "What? I no understand!" Peering, trying to assess it. He pushed a button, put his call on hold, raised a hand to say a word but –

Aimée closed in screaming, "You're a putrid pain, you! Breaking my heart! Not an ounce of pity in your *maudite* soul!" Lambert skipped, oblivious and chanting, and hopped coolly over Marco's leash. Beautiful! But the dog was frantic. The two mothers screamed and wailed. And Milli didn't miss a beat, stony, grim, pegging Chimmy's dripping undershirt and sending it off with another hideous metallic shriek. More drops fell through the grate.

Fausto wiped his arm, yelled, "I talk later!" and cut his call. Then Marco lunged for the stairs and Brigitte jolted, letting out a wrenching matronly moan.

Fausto sat there looking vexed. He seemed to take it personally. We could see it in his bleary, baffled eyes. Yes, exactly according to plan, we thought.

It was disgusting that an 83-year old man would stoop to fencing stolen bikes.

We knew he did it because he was lonely, that missing Angelina had made him lose his mind. But loneliness is no excuse, God knows, and worse, he thought he was just so smart. We had endured it since spring, watched him strutting on the corner and making plans with junkies, listened to him brag about his dirty deals in the *dépanneur* as we lined up to pay for our smokes and beer. The police had been alerted, but they were useless.

That day Martine was in her pool on the other side of Fausto's other fence, floating in her one-piece suit, blue and pink and massive, a floral whale – and languid, lovely, irresistible. And deadly. Aimée hysterical? Brigitte collapsing? Milli in retreat from Chim's weird prayer? All a front. The girls had planned a hit and today would be the day. If not, tomorrow we would see a junkie rolling up with another bike. We would know there was another child somewhere in the quarter wondering why the world's so rotten, another sour citizen who'd ridden to work with real conviction, who'd honestly believed in being green. Enough! Today Fausto would pay for abetting scummy bike thieves.

Today was perfect, what with Lambert skipping, counting, "*One for sorrow, Two for mirth,*" and Aimée's headache spiking up her venom, "You'll pay for this! You'll burn in hell, you!"

And with Brigitte reaching out to Milli through the manic din of Marco's barking, tragic, the only mother in this world who's ever been left alone, imploring – did they wash the children's things at noon at camp? And again after supper? It was unjust and cruel that she should have to live with this emptiness, this unrequited need to keep her baby clean! And with Milli's martyred heart so numb. A month at camp was nothing. Chimmy was in China for a *year* and this is what he brings me! A prayer?

Our ears closed tight as a pair of Milli's panties sailed away with a searing screech.

Met by another soulful groan from Milli's kitchen. You'd think Chim was having sex with God in there. Well, Chim's ecstasy was private and sure: we respected that. But humidity muddles everything and everyone was wondering as Brigitte keened and Aimée cursed and Milli pegged another dripping pantaloon. And Fausto shifted in his chair.

Fausto tried to signal Milli but she was locked on auto-drive, her eyes remained dead blank. Not Brigitte's crying, nor Marco's fury, nor Aimée's crazy bile - none of it could touch her, wringing water, pegging laundry, extending the malignant line.

Nor Chim's surreal incantation, spooling eerie counterpoint into the dead-still air.

We recalled the day Chim first got a ladder, fixed the spool to the poplar tree and ran the line across. Working with Milli, man and wife – Chimmy up the ladder issuing instructions in choppy Cantonese to Milli on the balcony, Fausto and Angelina watching with the rest of us, bemused at how they worked together in a code we couldn't know. Maybe Fausto remembered too. With each shattering bray of screeching metal, we were sure we saw a twinge of memory creasing his decrepit gaze.

Fausto had mourned for Angelina. There was dignity in that. Now he was a gangster. It may have been that woman's scheme, the one he paid to shop and clean. Whatever. If Angelina could come back from heaven, she'd kick his bike-stealing ass up and down the alley. But Angelina could not come back. Lonely? The only way to halt this travesty was to send Fausto back to *her*. But everything depended on Martine.

Her pool was barely bigger than a bathtub in her tiny square of yard.

She filled it fully, wallowing, fulsome and diabolical like the wife of Moby Dick.

Now Aimée's insane complaining carried apoplectic spit, screeching her life's anger at Lambert. "God's got no time for boys like you! None! None! *Sacristie!*"

We knew it was not the boy; it was the gormless man who had made him, then walked away. But a day like that will blur the lines and the little boy was all she had. Lambert was skipping there in front of Fausto as Milli wrung a woolen sock and Brigitte's pain went ultra-*uber* - terrible tremors, sorrowful shaking, tears the size of rain drops flying, and Marco was up on his hind legs, howling haunted dog replies to Chim.

We saw Fausto nodding vaguely. Was he getting it? Was he understanding? For a moment Fausto looked at his phone, dumbly wondering who to call, needing it to ring and separate him from the festering inferno. We knew he realized he was deep in sin, but did he know that he was doomed? He turned fully in his chair. We watched him peering grossly at Martine – enormous and ineluctable, shifting in the pleasure of her water.

We were thinking, come on, Fausto, don't resist, no point trying. Everyone longs to repose in coolness, in the coolness of the Good! We know you crave that comfort. We know you'll feel better in the end. Needful Fausto, neurotic cacophony mounting round him, random water dripping, pricking at his wretched head. He gazed so mutely, but his need was like a scream. Eh, Fausto? Isn't it true? Can you save yourself, old man?

Martine rolled fetchingly. She rolled and waved an arm. Beckoning?

Fausto saw it, no way to hide it. He felt it deep in his encrusted heart: Martine displacing tons of water with one movement of her pillowy arm.

Is loneliness wrong? Fencing stolen bikes definitely is. Perhaps Fausto could have escaped inside to his own private coolness, those pictures of Angelina on the table by their bed. Maybe. If he'd been thinking straighter. But the scathing noise, the horrendous heat – Fausto went the other way as Martine went rolling in her pool. He hitched his pants, hobbled down his steps and went scrambling over the fence, a grotesque and hoary goat, and flew straight at her. Poor Martine.

Who reacted as any woman would, using her natural advantage, the wondrous size that had kept her lonely *her entire life*, to pin Fausto down till he was subdued. Forever.

The police arrived and heard all about the old man losing control and attacking Martine while she was bathing. When pressed for details, the witnesses listed their emotions, their deepest feelings on a dreadful, stifling day. And Chim came out on the balcony, wagging a righteous finger, declaiming, "This is exactly why I pray!"

Lambert fed Marco something from his pocket and he hushed.

Which was lucky because one officer had drawn his gun.

Martine remained in her pool, withdrawn, perfunctory, sullen, beside the bobbing body. It made the authorities nervous. You could see the same thing getting to them that got to Fausto – though it's a matter of degree: Fausto had got the first degree, and he'd paid the ultimate price. But no one said a word about stolen bikes or junkie thieves, and it was all too complicated for sweaty, flustered cops, what with the godawful heat. So we watched the *Urgences Santé* guys drag him out, careful not to disturb Martine where she floated, wary, looking mean. Then they loaded him in their truck and left the alley. They didn't bother with the siren. No point. And one small blessing after all that noise.

Yes, a sad end for a used-to-be-decent man.

You could only hope Angelina's love would get him into heaven.

Then Milli took her basket and went inside with Chim. Brigitte took Marco and went for a walk. Aimée popped a pill and rubbed her temples. "Come on, *cher*, it's over."

"*Five for heaven, Six for hell* . . ." Lambert skipped home behind his mother.

It was not till six o'clock that we heard Martine, "Oof!" - groaning, gigantic as she hauled herself out of her pool. And we could see her there by her kitchen door, alone, massively lonely, carefully drying her voluptuous skin.

Cocoon

Emily Ursuliak

When you were a little girl your father gave you a butterfly net, because watching butterflies was never enough. They were always too fast for the eye to focus on, barely pausing before flitting away again, a flash of colour in the corner of your eye. But the net became a fabric cage to swoosh down over them. Slowly. Patiently. Urge them into the waiting jam jar stuffed with grass and dead leaves. Then put on the lid spotted with tiny perforations to keep them alive, and they would beat at the glass with their wings. As captured things, they were almost still enough to admire.

Those twitching wings, a memory of their iridescence warped behind the thick glass, are conjured up with the first step into the gallery. It's not apparent why. Maybe the girl in the monarch yellow dress ahead of you with those fake eyelashes batting? But the memory comes anyway, despite the fact that you stand in a foreign country, an eight-hour flight and an ocean between you and home.

You'd been retired long enough when you told Ed about wanting to go to London to see the art galleries. He helped plan every detail. Even bought a map and traced all the routes. You wouldn't have had the guts to go otherwise, what with Ed not being able to come along because of work. All the planning and scheduling he did helped calm you, or that's what you had both decided to agree on over the years. It was easier to agree that Ed's intentions produced his desired result than to think about how they really made you feel.

Ed hadn't planned for this gallery though. It was at the far side of the park you just happened to be walking through. The sign said INSTITUTE OF CONTEMPORARY ART. Sounded legitimate enough for a look inside, at least. The pale girl at the counter had mentioned the exhibit opening party that night. Exciting work by new artists! Tickets had to be purchased in advance and so you'd bought one. Looked at it as you sat on the grass outside afterwards. A first little unplanned adventure. It would be something to call Ed and tell him about how this place was making you a new person.

The warm flush of pride lingered all day until evening had come, and here you were, in the center of the gallery, old enough to be everyone else's mother. All of them wearing finely tailored clothes in rich fabrics – sleek and looking like super models – not in a wrinkled summer dress like yours that you'd bought at the Bay and thought would be nice enough for an impromptu step into an unpredictable evening. And all the girls with skinny, muscular arms, not flabby, sagging skin. This is what you get for trying to do something spontaneous. For veering off the route Ed had set.

The eccentric architecture of this huge room gives the feeling of being trapped in some massive creature's ribcage. The other galleries were sensible and dignified – solid brick buildings with a kind of classical architecture you could put your trust in. When you went inside, there were all kinds of people: polished business men in suits, squat, chubby tourists in khaki shorts, elderly ladies with penciled-on eyebrows and grubby-faced little children wandering around with their teachers. Easier to blend in there and think about the paintings instead of yourself. There was the satisfying regurgitation of solid facts that spewed into your mind at every familiar painting: name of the artist, time-period, social context, style. So thrilling to see things from the textbooks and the lectures you went to. You walked by the ones you didn't recognize because there was so much to see and no time to waste on unfamiliar things.

If only there had been someone with you, so you could tell them about all these things. Tell them that you remembered learning about this or that painter in your classes. Ed was never that interested in hearing about art back when you were at the college, but he liked that you went. It gave you a new purpose, he said, and he talked about how you were the kind of person who would fall apart without structure. That you needed something to engage you and keep you focused. When there was no job to go to anymore, at first you didn't wake up till the afternoon and sat in the living room, feeling empty in your pajamas. Not caring that you hadn't brushed your teeth or hair. Not caring what you looked like.

You weren't even sure why you'd picked art history of all things. Maybe it was all the trips to the museum with Grandma as a little girl, seeing paintings on the walls after the butterflies. Those were the best trips, away from Mom who always made you nervous. Grandma made you feel safe again. She had a soft voice and wasn't always yelling about the mud you tracked into the hallway, or the toys you forgot to pick up. It was your special time together. Her plump hand grasped yours and led you to your favorite exhibit; you'd press your nose up to the glass to look at the frozen wings shining in blue and yellow and orange. They always made the ones you had back at home in jars look so dull. It was disappointing having to leave them, but you and Grandma had a deal. She always wanted to look at the paintings on the other side of the building and you'd trail along behind, bored and wanting to go back to your butterflies. She tried to explain what she loved about them to you, but you could never listen for long. Paintings were in the adult world, and maybe that's why you'd picked them. Leaving the glittering, frozen wings behind for something more mature.

Art was intimidating, a reflection of all the higher things you hadn't learned about because there was no reason to go to university or college. You found yourself settling into the first place that would employ you coming out of school: a bank with a dependable, bimonthly cheque and the possibility of climbing the rungs at a small branch. Security. Wasn't it what everyone looked for? But then there were doubts. All this stability and no room for anything exciting to happen. The answer arrived with the idea of art history classes. Something that was once intimidating could become manageable with all the right facts and information, and the grades you'd got on all those multiple choice tests seemed to back it up. You understood art.

One of the finer things in life became more approachable. Conversations at dinner parties held the potential of impressing the other guests, if the right names or paintings were mentioned. Sophistication was within reach.

Walk across the room thinking of all the "A's" marked on your test papers. Even the section on modern art had been easy to conquer: attaching names to dates, to styles, and intent, and different art movements. There was nothing in this gallery that could make you feel that old self - the middle-aged, first year student panting to keep up with the quick, twenty-something minds that didn't know about the crippling idea of security. You'd triumphed over that self, spending long hours over your desk, memorizing obsessively. Even if you didn't know the artist, the gallery always referenced those who came before them, didn't they? And that's what you're sure you'll find when you come to the first room.

Cross the threshold, look to the walls, expecting to see something, but they meet you with a blank, white gaze. What kind of gallery doesn't have the art on the walls? The floor is white too. Apparently that's where you're meant to look because that's where everyone else has directed their eyes.

This has to be some kind of joke. Garbage is strewn over the floor: cereal boxes, tin cans, beer bottles, crumpled paper. The only thing that could possibly have taken any kind of effort is that all the garbage has been spray-painted black. The people don't look shocked though; they aren't laughing and saying how ridiculous it is. They stare intently at the trash on the floor like they see something that you can't. It's as if by being fresh and young they can see more than some old woman in the room with them.

Rack your brains for any kind of reference to previous artists: nothing. The only thing that comes to mind is that this must be an installation. You have a faint memory of the professor showing pictures and talking about how the whole room became a piece of art. If only you'd taken better notes, this would probably make sense.

The groups of young people are discussing the work intently. One of them probably knows the artist and understands. The trick is to eavesdrop without being obvious because it would be terrible if they found out and discovered your ignorance.

Hover around a group of boys with wildly sculpted hair and sharp, clever faces. One holds court, louder and cockier. He's a kind of ringleader whom the rest of them respect.

"It's about our ultimate doom," he says. "We'll cover all the pure, white space, like this room, with shit until we annihilate ourselves."

What is it with kids, always using swearwords as if it's some way of giving them an edge? Beyond the foul language, there's a deep understanding though, a meaning that you couldn't manage to get from looking at the garbage. Where did that come from, that kind of information? Did he go to school with the artist and watch him develop his work? Why does he know these things and you don't? Two full years of art history have absolutely no relevance here.

The butterflies had turned out the same though, hadn't they? As a teenager, you'd memorized all the names of the ones in the museum, learned about their life-cycles.

When Grandma came with you again, she smiled and made you feel smart, for a little while at least, as she listened to you babbling on about them.

Then she asked you which one was your favorite, and you didn't know. "Surely," she said, "after so many years you must know which one you like the best?"

But you'd never thought of them that way. You couldn't remember if there had ever been a favorite. And then as you'd left the museum, a butterfly had flitted past the two of you. Small and brown, it hesitated for a moment on the face of a dandelion.

Grandma asked if you knew what that one was called, but you didn't recognize it from the museum. The ones in the glass cases were the only ones you'd bothered to learn anything about; if the butterfly wasn't in the museum,   then it wasn't important enough. You'd long stopped trying to catch butterflies in the backyard.

A hot flush had crept over your face, a feeling all too familiar, and you couldn't tell her and the shame had never left and you never went to look at the butterflies again. There was no longer any point in reading about them, and talking about them because they had become just another thing that made you feel stupid, that made you feel like Mom was right about you. It didn't matter how many facts were memorized because you weren't smart enough to really get it.

The only difference between then and now was that you'd paid good money for this ticket and there was no home to go back to right now, only the hideous room with the clashing decor and threadbare sheets in the run-down hotel. There were four more days left before the plane ride home. Any more deviations from Ed's plan would lead to wandering around aimlessly seeing nothing interesting and would most likely get you lost. And what would've been the point of taking all those classes? No, you can do this. You need to figure it out, so you return once again to scanning the room, looking for answers from the beautiful people. And then, just over there, a girl with dreadlocks and a scarf wrapped around her head and something in her hand. It's a pamphlet. They must have been available in the center of the gallery and you just missed getting one.

A warm buzz of blending voices fills the main room. It's a good thing that you can't pick out any individual conversations. No doubt they would be too intelligent to understand. At the far end of the room there's a table with a girl in a daffodil yellow dress who is handing out the pamphlets. A wave of relief flows down your shoulders and right to the tips of your fingers.

"Wine, madame?" A waiter from the bar behind that you didn't notice. Nod and say yes before you quite know what you're doing. As you reach out to take the glass, your hand is shaking, but it stops as you grab hold - as if having the glass cupped elegantly in your palm makes you somehow fit in. Take a long, deep sip and feel it, dry and sour, sliding down your throat, then freeze with the glass at your lips. When was the last time you even drank? A year ago? It was that dinner party awhile back and you'd wanted to erase it right out of your head. That was really why you always asked for water at these occasions now. You hadn't even thought you'd had much, but Ed said that you'd talked louder and louder and laughed like a hyena, but the worst part can't be forgotten.

You'd taken a sip and a man had told a joke, was it Peter, or Jeremy? You were taking a sip and you tried, God how you'd tried to hold back, but it was hilarious what he'd said, or at least you thought it was, and you tried to laugh, and then there was the burn of the wine and you snorting and the wine streaming from your nose and all over the white table cloth.

The room was silent. Everybody stared.

They pretended to go back to their conversations as you frantically dabbed at your face and the tablecloth with the napkin, but you knew they were thinking how disgusting you were, couldn't hold your liquor and now you've shot it out your nose all over Ellen's expensive tablecloth. Everyone knows how red wine stains. You never dared go back to Ellen and Peter's after that, and swore never to touch alcohol again. Ed thought it was hilarious, but he couldn't understand.

Look at the glass of wine in your hand. Maybe just this one time you can get away with it. You've already made the decision to stay, and anyways you're in London. You're far away from home, and if you make a fool of yourself in front of these invulnerable people, you'll never see them again. Down the rest of the wine in four gulps and return the empty glass to a shocked waiter.

You move smoothly through the throngs to the girl at the table. She smiles and hands you this thin booklet of paper, almost insubstantial really, but it holds everything you need. Now you can see the last two exhibits and it'll all make sense. And if someone else is alone and standing nearby, you can say to them, did you know that the artist studied at such and such place and was inspired by the work of so and so? How they will look at you with admiration and think - there is a classy, sophisticated, older woman. With the pamphlet in your hand, feel a smile spreading across your cheeks that suddenly feel flushed with happiness, or maybe the wine.

Turn quickly to head to the next room and realize it's definitely the wine. Move your head from left to right and notice how it takes a second for your eyeballs to catch up, everything all blurry in between. Right in the center of your chest, by your heart, there's something bubbling, trying to rise out through your lips, maybe a giggle because you must look very silly with your head swaying from side to side like that. You try to snap out of it and weave through people, sometimes sliding against silk dresses or rubbing against the abrasive wool of a suit, like the lick of a cat's tongue.

A short, twisting hallway leads into the next exhibit, and there are no lights in the room, but the hollow beams spill from the entrance into what feels like a massive cave. Blink. Eyes trying to make out shapes in the thick darkness. It takes longer, but finally you see. There's a hoard of chairs in the middle of the room and all around are hundreds of speakers piping haunting violin music. The chairs are grouped around a gramophone barely lit by a soft spotlight. People move towards the chairs and start sitting down. You follow, feeling like you're swimming towards your chair through the heavy air.

Remember the pamphlet as you take your seat, and unfold it, squinting in the dusk of the room. But the writing won't speak to you; your eyes wander from side to side, unable to fix on one spot.

"You're going to have a hard time reading that in here," says a voice beside you. It's the dreadlock girl from before and she's smiling at you. "Besides, what's in there is just a bunch of over-intellectual rubbish, and how can you experience anything if you're reading instead of feeling what happens in here?" She pounds her fist to her chest lightly, and you find yourself giggling, your cheeks feeling numb. She laughs a bit too, her pale blue eyes almost seeming to glow in the darkness. And then the music swells until the whole room feels as though it's vibrating and the pale blue eyes close.

The other people have mostly closed their eyes too, but you haven't yet. You like this feeling of being a room full of people with their eyes closed. It feels so intimate, as though you're all going to sleep together in these chairs in this big cave.

Then the music dies, the room ceases to vibrate and the light on the gramophone comes up. The thin hollow voice of a woman begins to speak. You imagine her soul trapped inside the curving tunnel of the gramophone like a genie in a bottle. She begins telling of a dream she had: a circus with wild, demon-like people as performers with faces like twisted masks and long, bony fingers that beckon you into the tent. As she fills in the life of her dream, the speakers begin to tell the story with sounds. Around the circle of chairs, a full brass band marches. As they walk around you playing their instruments, you can hear their footsteps. The room becomes a space full of ghosts that you trace through their noise as the woman keeps telling the shifting tale of where her dream is taking you next.

You sit, the heavy weight of your arms dropping towards the floor. You've lost your purse somewhere by your feet, but it doesn't matter. The sounds of the dream and the voice of the woman flow in and out of your ears, the story filling you with dread at times, awe at others. Close your eyes finally, like the rest, as the woman's story begins to draw to a close. She tells you of a beautiful garden full of thousands of birds that swoop and dive around, but the birds are butterflies to you and you alone. They flit around in serpentine patterns to match the spinning of your mind, and there is a swelling within you of something that's too much, that's unknown. A great understanding that has no words, but touches you through the sound of thousands of tiny wings beating the air, gossamer wings free from the steel hold of pins. Realize that the person you hear sobbing is yourself, mascara and foundation running into hands cupped against your sticky face. There's the wet tickle of your nose running and dripping. You wipe it with the back of your hand, something you haven't done since you were a child.

Ave Maria

Chris LaMay-West

I Hail Mary

One of my favorite things about the Red Devil Lounge is the velvety glow that suffuses the dim interior. Warm, enveloping and a touch Satanic. That's where I am the night I first see Mary. I'm sitting at the far end of the long bar on a Thursday evening, running my hand over the lacquer of the wooden countertop. I like the glide of its smoothness along my hands almost as much as I love the catch and abrasion of the rough part where the varnish has worn through.

My gaze is down toward the far end of the bar, but it's not about Mary. I'm just trying to catch the eye of the bartender, a slim blonde pixie in braided pigtails, to focus her attention on my plight before the band starts up. As uncomfortable as I can get in a crowd without some form of sedation, beerlessness just won't do. Mary's in my line of sight, though, directly opposite me on the other end of the bar, and she thinks I'm looking at her. She smiles.

I don't know it's Mary yet; we've never met. What I do know is that this redhead at the end of the bar gives me a big radiant smile, so warm and inviting that I glance to my right and left to find the person the smile is intended for. There's no one there but me. She laughs and smiles again. I look at the smartly styled, reddish brown bob of her hair, the turquoise and silver necklace against her freckled neck, her blue silk blouse unbuttoned over her white tank top to reveal the fullness of body that women get in their thirties, sexier by far than any twenty year-old could hope for.

This woman is looking at me? Maybe I should—

"What can I get for you?"

I shake my head and readjust my vision on the bartender now in front of me. I didn't even see her approach. She tilts her head and raises an eyebrow. I realize she's starting to do the 'Is this a problem drunk customer, or just a slow-witted guy?' calculation in her head. I'd better say something.

"Yeah, sorry. Can I get a Red Hook?"

Satisfied that I'm okay, she proceeds to tap the draught and brings me back a bubbling, golden red cylinder. I take a long, slow sip, savoring the rich, buttery taste, and try again to catch sight of the woman at the end of the bar. To my surprise, her gaze is fixed on me. She's smiling. I smile back, the kind of smile someone gives at a ballgame when they realize the camera's found them and their picture is up on the big screen. She raises her wine glass and laughs; then she turns and talks to a friend next to her, part of what seems to be a large group she's with.

To my relief, the sound of the band tuning up on the stage behind me gives me an excuse to turn away from this crimson-haired enchantress while I collect my wits. I don't think I'm a bad-looking guy, exactly. But inside, I'm still too much of a grade school nerd to think of myself as good-looking. With her wine and friends and silk top, she should be on a Showtime series. I'm more like the Sci-Fi Channel. Or Animal Planet.

Even so, I glance back between each song to see if she's still there.

Slick New York transplants to the west coast, the band on stage is starting an instrumental; I know from previous shows that this means they're about to take a break. Which means about thirty minutes with no music to distract me, and I know from my backward glances that she's still at the end of the bar. My mind races.

I should do something, right? One of the reasons I started coming to these monthly shows here at the Red Devil was to learn how to get out again, a year after my divorce from my college sweetheart. This is what people do in big cities, isn't it?

The bald lead guitarist switches to the electric violin, a sure sign that the end is near. Okay, time to think. Surely I can't just go up to her in the midst of a group of friends like that. If only there was some way to reach her one-on-one without that embarrassment. The feedback-laden cacophony of serrated screeches on stage reaches its height. Think, think, think—

"Thank you, and we'll be back after the break! Remember to buy drinks, and tip your bartender!"

Yes! I can buy her a drink; have the bartender send it over to her. Genius! Just as I wheel around to execute my plan, I see her group of friends getting their things together to leave. Dammit! She must feel the sheer wattage of the intense dismay I pour toward her because she glances up from her purse-contents shuffling and looks me straight in the eye. She picks up her coat off the stool, beams a radiant smile my way and waves before turning to leave. On the way out the door, she looks over her shoulder and smiles a sly smile.

Wow. It's almost better that I just have that fact of her gaze, pristine and assured, with no need to follow through.

Almost.

II Full of Grace

The next morning at work is pervaded by a sandpaper-rubbing-inside-my-skull after-effect of the two screwdrivers I had after she left and an old, familiar self-loathing. How did I let her get past me? I was like a kid with his back against the wall at the sixth grade dance, watching a girl from across the room. Waiting all night to get up the nerve, only to finally decide to do it on the last song, by which time she's out on the floor with someone else.

Same shit twenty years later, and this kind of cowardice is meant to be decisive. You have to act in the moment, or not at all. There are no do-overs. Except that technology has revoked this age-old condition. On online message boards, ships that passed in the night and then thought better of it can send up flares to each other. We call this modern Redeemer of Lost Causes the "Missed Connections" section of Craigslist.

Inside the grayish white walls of my cubicle, the idea germinates in my head all morning. It's silly, I tell myself. These things never work. All through a morning spent wrestling with spreadsheets, I open the web browser for the Craigslist site, and then close it again. No, it won't work. But you can never really give up the idea of repenting for past sins, can you? Here it is, that promise, personified in blinking electronic form. Just before lunch, I reopen the site and my shaky hands find their way to the keyboard.

(M4F) Seeking the redhead at the bar at the Red Devil Lounge, Thursday night...

...around 9PM. I was the guy you were smiling at, brown hair and beard in the Hawaiian shirt, at the end of the bar. I'm kicking myself for not going over and talking to you before you left. It seems ridiculous to try to make up for it now, but maybe there's a chance. Are you you? Am I me? If so, maybe drop me a line, and we can continue our "conversation"...

I rewrite the paragraph five times. My last move is to cut the "maybe" in the last line. I think I read somewhere that women like confidence and decisiveness.

There's no doubt in my mind that I'm going to do it, but there's still a lurch inside when I click the **PUBLISH** button. Or is my head just swimming from the neon blue radiation of my computer monitor? Maybe this is what it feels like to be bold, to take a risk. Yeah, big risk. The most likely response to this posting is nothing. Eternal silence.

Even so, I hit **REFRESH** on my e-mail inbox every few seconds.

It probably hasn't even posted yet. I think it takes about ten to fifteen minutes. I decide that I need a change of venue. If anything, my fuzzy-headedness is probably hunger.

Fifteen minutes later, this hypothesis seems entirely borne out as I sit waiting for my shrimp burrito to cool in Flor de Guadalupe. I chew on their preternaturally good chips and rest my eyes on the bright red floral patterns that bloom where the strips of aquamarine tile on the walls intersect. Now I just feel silly about the whole thing. Some things are lost, and you can't get them back. I need to learn how to approach women in real time. Lesson learned.

After lunch, I actually feel upbeat as I take a walk around the sunny brick plaza fronting my office. I stare up at the wild blue of the sky, and it seems like a promise of open space and possibility. Next time. Next time this happens, I'll talk to her, whoever she is. Maybe she will even be Mary next time. I could go back to the Red Devil Lounge next Thursday. She might be there.

By the time I get back to my cubicle, I'm settled enough that I barely jump each time the blinking little teal box at the bottom of the screen tells me I have a new message in my inbox.

Book Club Next Selection.

Pete from my book club informs us that, next time, we're reading a novel about a kid who represents mathematics trapped on a train with a talking tiger. Or something like that.

What time is the movie tomorrow?

I'm seeing an art film tomorrow afternoon with Julie, a friend from my previous job who I have a probable, never-to-be-expressed crush on.

Mom's birthday - DON'T FORGET!

I can't help but smirk at the idea of my younger brother Jared, a college dropout and live-at-home, underemployed dishwasher, thinking he needs to remind *me* about the upcoming event.

By the end of the day, so many similarly inconsequential messages have gone by that I don't even stir when the icon blinks again.

Re: Seeking the redhead at the bar at the Red Devil
Lounge, Thursday night…

What? I'm in such haste to open up the message that I accidentally shut down my e-mail while trying to click through. Damn! The agonizing seconds it takes to boot back up tick past on the wall clock. There's a rush in my chest and a pleasant numbness in the center of my head as the window finally blooms into full size.

The first line of the message reads: *Her name is Mary.*

III The Lord is With You

The late morning light that streams in through frayed yellow curtains gives the living room a butterscotch glow. A mug of coffee steams on the little table in front of me, next to my crossed feet while I steam, in an altogether different sense, on the couch. I boot up my laptop and, for what seems like the hundredth time since yesterday, reread the message:

re : Seeking the redhead at the bar at the Red Devil
Lounge, Thursday night…

Her name is Mary. I'm her friend, I was there with her. I
was kind of pissed at her for the way she was acting. You
should know that she has a boyfriend. That being said,
you both seem to be into it, so who am I to judge? I won't
give you her e-mail. If you really want to pursue it, you
can find it out for yourself. She works in the Admin.
Department for the SF Public Library. You can find her
name in their latest annual report. The rest is up to you.

I'm tempted to search the library's website again, also for the hundredth time since yesterday, but I know there's no personal information there. I shut down my computer and take a long sip of coffee. As I watch the sickeningly sweet hazelnut creamer swirl around in a golden brown arc, I laugh at the absurdity of the idea running through my mind. The main branch of the library is right by where I'm meeting Julie for the movie. I could swing by there on the way…

What kind of friend would send that message anyway? I unplug the computer and head into the kitchen. It can't be someone who knows her; it must be some sort of practical joke. I dump the coffee down the drain and scrub the mug with a soapy yellowish green sponge. This is stupid; I've compounded the original sin of not talking to her with the obsession over trying to track her down. I sit back down on the couch. She has a boyfriend, for God's sake! I tap my foot against the coffee table.

At last, I come to a decision: I don't have to decide what to do now. I just have to get out the door and on the bus in time to meet Julie. I can always make up my mind on the way.

My mind is no closer to being made up thirty minutes later when I transfer on to the second line, the one that runs past the library's main branch and then a few blocks further on to the theatre. I sit while the bus gets closer. There's time to stop there first. There's also time to go straight to the theatre, get a cup of coffee and mellow out before Julie gets there. Only one of those options causes my heart to rush a little too fast and makes me feel queasy inside. That alone should tell me what to do.

Up next I see the gold glint of the city hall's dome, the massive concrete cube of the library squatting to one side behind it. I bounce back and forth against the hard orange and brown plastic seat as the bus lurches to a stop. I tuck my hands under my legs. The procession of people getting on and off seems interminable, but the bus finally rumbles to a start again and heads further up the street.

Good, yes, I did nothing! But as I step off the bus in front of the movie theatre, the thought hits me: Is this the kind of nothing I did in the bar? Maybe this is my chance to make up for that, and I'm letting it slip away. So what if she has a boyfriend, and this is probably all a joke. Maybe fate has handed me this opportunity and will be with me if I seize it. Fortune favours the bold! With a glance at my watch to confirm that there's time, I turn on my heels and hurry back down the street toward the library.

With a racing heart, I mount the granite steps to the heavy front doors. Crazy, this is crazy! My eyes take a second to adjust to the contrast between the dim interior of the main lobby and the golden waterfall of sunshine pouring in through the skylights. The main branch of the San Francisco Public Library is a giant homeless shelter that happens to contain books; the faint whiff of unwashed bodies that wafts my way upon entering the building makes me reconsider the whole venture.

As I glance around the imposing stone chamber, I realize that I don't know exactly how to go about looking for the annual report. Will there be a stack of them on a table next to the door? Some type of prominently displayed metal stand? My footsteps resound in metallic echoes, marking my slow orbit of the lobby. As I circle like some kind of deranged shark, a thin-lipped, silver-haired librarian casts occasional suspicious glances my way from the main desk. I should do something to allay her concern. Like say, "Hi, do you know Mary?"

Okay, probably not that. Instead I say nothing, then walk up to the desk and stand in front of the librarian for several long seconds before she looks up again. The crisp orange silk of the scarf around her neck and glint of her wire-framed glasses seem to put me in my place before she even speaks.

"Can I help you?"

"Yes, I'm ... uh ..." I gulp. A residual fear of stern librarians from the past rises to the surface. "I'm looking for the library's annual report. I'm doing some research on non-profits."

As it happens, there is a stack of annual reports right behind the counter. She produces one for me without fanfare or admonishment. I mumble my thanks and hurry to the door. Blinking at the sun outside, I run a finger down the table of contents. Overview. Branches. What the hell? *Doing research on nonprofits?* African Department. Friends of the Library. Am I really so sheepish about trying to meet this girl that I have to make up gratuitous lies to address questions no one has even asked? Project Read. Administration. What is lying anyway - a venal sin or a mortal sin? Wait, administration!

I fumble through the pages, and there she is - in a little black and white box instead of the golden glow of the bar - but with the same smile. Mary O'Neil, Marketing & Public Relations. Fortune must be with me after all because now I have a name.

IV: Blessed Are You Among Women

moniel@sfpl.org? That, or maryo@sfpl.org are the most likely variants. I lean back in my chair with a sigh on Monday morning. The green "X" of the Excel icon at the bottom of the screen flickers in a multiple kilohertz per second rebuke for the time I'm wasting. Mary.oneil@sfpl.org? That's a distinct possibility. I know the domain name is right; I combed the website first thing when I got in. That, however, was no help in determining the naming convention; all they had was a web-enabled contact form without any addresses. Looking for library press releases with her name on them was similarly fruitless.

Underscore! It could be mary_oneil@sfpl.org. Maybe I should devote less time to trying to guess the address and more time to drafting the—

"Hey! Have you signed the card?"

Lourdes laughs as I thump back in my chair after a startled leap, her smile all the more dazzling in its contrast with her golden brown cheeks. Lourdes Avilla, executive assistant to our CEO, is passing around his birthday card hidden in a manila folder. I look at the front of the card, a scene of a mountain lake nestled in pine-covered hills, before scribbling something. I take care not to smudge the ink with my hands as I shut the card. I'm sure my palms are at least slightly sweaty.

"Do you think there's any chance we've kept this secret?" I glance around with wide, exaggerated eyes as I hand it back to her, hoping to get her to laugh. I'm rewarded by her glowing dimples.

"Ha! Probably not, but you have to keep up appearances. Catch you later!"

I nod and watch the sashay of her pleasantly thick hips as she heads down the hallway toward the next name on her checklist. It's so easy to talk with her, just calm and normal. For the millionth time, I think about asking her to lunch. But it'd be weird and awkward when she said no, and then I'd have to see her around the office all the time and…

I shake myself out of my reverie and remember that I have business to attend to.

Forty minutes of composition later, with many a surreptitious glance around to make sure nobody realizes how derelict I'm being, I'm ready to send.

> *Mary,*
>
> *I know this must seem pretty random, but I'm the guy you were smiling at Thursday night at the Red Devil Lounge. I felt like such an idiot for not talking to you then! I posted an ad on Craigslist, hoping to have a second chance. Somebody who said they were a friend of yours wrote back and told me where you worked. They told me you have a boyfriend, but you seemed to be interested. So I*

figured, well, I'd give it a try. Oh man, this is
embarrassing! I swear I don't do this kind of thing
normally, but I feel like there's something about you. So if
you are interested, or just want to have the misadventure
of meeting for lunch sometime, I'd love to talk to you.

Reading it over, I grimace - could there be any more qualifiers in there? Still, this is as good as it's going to get. I'd better send it before I lose my nerve.

Immediately after I hit **SEND** on the fourth and final permutation of possible addresses, I go to lunch. At this point, I know better than to think I'll do anything but compulsively check and recheck email if I stay at my desk. I get a sandwich at a takeout deli and eat it on a bench in a little rooftop garden atop one of the downtown office buildings. I breathe deeply and watch the light filter through the translucent green leaves of the tree above the bench, and the fever that's overtaken me in the past few days seems to clear.

Probably all these messages will bounce back. There'll be nothing more I can do, and maybe I can just forget all this silliness. It's a nice thought.

Not so nice that I don't check my inbox the second I get back to the office. I see several messages in a row with the title *"failure notice."* Three, not four. I move my mouse with a jerky hand to scan the details. So much for the fever abating. And sure enough, three of the tries failed, but one made it through. Or at least it hasn't bounced back yet. I take a deep breath to calm the excited rush that flutters in my chest.

Okay, it went to her. So what? Most likely, she will never respond, and that will be that.

My supposed satisfaction with comfortable disappointment is belied by the adrenaline surge every time I see a new message update flash at the bottom of my screen. It's all nothing upon nothing until two hours later, a message appears with the title *"Miss Adventure"*. The sick-excited chemical burst in my stomach that I've come to know so well in the last four days surges anew as I open the message.

> *Well hello there - what a sweet message! I do indeed*
> *remember you. It's probably my friend Bernadette who*
> *wrote to you. Funny. She doesn't think I should flirt in my*
> *situation even though… Okay, it's my turn to feel*
> *embarrassed now. The thing is, I do have a boyfriend,*
> *and I'm not looking to change that, but we have an*
> *arrangement. As long as the other person says it's okay,*
> *we can see other people sometimes. How's that for*
> *misadventure? Ha! God, this must seem weird to you.*
> *But I felt something too, and I'd be interested in exploring*
> *that. If this doesn't shock or offend you, write me back.*
>
> *Mary*

As I read and reread her message, the flutter inside my stomach kicks into a more acid gear. I like the vaguely corrosive feeling.

V: Blessed is the Fruit of Your Womb

By Wednesday afternoon, we've traded messages all week. I was surprised by how fast they turned up. The first twist was mine at the end of my first reply to her:

> *Maybe we could meet for Indian food, assuming you like*
> *spicy things. Although I guess if you want things really*

spicy, we could just order room service. Ha! Okay,
seriously, backing away from the innuendo, lunch would
be grand...

I typed the line with a vermilion surge behind my eyes and felt a heady rush when I hit SEND. It was so daring, not at all what I would do when talking to a real woman. The anonymous nature of our exchange seemed to embolden me. Even so, I retained enough of my primeval sense of unworthiness that I half expected her to say that my message made her uncomfortable, or even to break off our correspondence. Instead, a half hour later she replied:

Lunch would be lovely, and I adore Indian! Although I'm
half-tempted to take you up on that "room service" offer.
Have you ever met someone for a tryst like that? I can just
imagine us wrapped up in the sheets, you slipping
something tart into my mouth. I...

Things descended from there. By Wednesday, I started off my first message of the day:

I thought of you in the shower today. I turned the shower
head on the highest setting and let it rush over me as I got
more and more swollen until I couldn't stand it anymore
and...

Which brings me here, the title of her reply, "Let's meet tomorrow" flickering at the bottom of the screen. I click through to her message as smoothly as my over-excited reflexes allow:

God, your last message got me so hot! Do you want to
meet tomorrow and turn some of these words into
actions? I'll ask Peter tonight if it's okay. I know a

*storeroom here at work that nobody ever goes to. And I
don't even care if we get caught because the thought
makes me…*

I close my eyes, as if it will somehow become more real that way,
and the mauve after-image of the message on the screen floats before
me. This woman, this sexy, grown-up woman wants to be with *me*.
Wants me in a way that nobody has ever said they wanted me before. I
take a deep breath as the ghost image fades, open my eyes, and begin
to type.

The afternoon proceeds with a peculiar mix of heated flash and
excruciating crawl, made worse by the rounds of increasingly graphic
and heated messages we exchange. That night is even more fitful with
anticipation, but it all seems worth it when I get her message first thing
in the morning. She got the okay from her boyfriend. We'll meet at
12:30 in the Library Cafe.

I would expect the morning to last forever, but everything, charged
up with some mixture of guilt and excitement, seems to whiz by like a
dream. I feel a similar hallucinatory compression of time on the
elevator trip down to hail the taxi and on the bumpy ride to the library.
Everything surges inside, as if I were drunk. Holy cow, I'm really doing
this crazy thing! Adultery, I'm pretty sure, is a mortal sin. But it's not
like they're married. And I'm not cheating, she is!

Leaving nothing to chance, I get the taxi so early that I arrive
about fifteen minutes before we're supposed to meet. That's okay. I can
use the time to sit still and calm down. I make my way to the bright,
spare café downstairs from the lobby. Halogen lamps preside over pale

fake wood tables with aluminum trim as I scan the room for Mary. The setting seems a little bit too wholesome for whatever we're about to do.

That's what I'm thinking when she walks in.

My breath catches at the sight of Mary's sheer violet blouse and hip-hugging white jeans. Her wavy hair flips down over her face, and a series of silver bracelets shine against the ruddy freckled gold of her arm. She glimpses at the room, then smiles and waves when she sees me, like we're friends who meet for lunch all the time. She heads my way in quick, round strides and slides into the chair opposite me, eyes atwinkle.

"Yep, you're as cute as I remember. Are you still up for this?" I decide I like how warm and full her voice is; it has just the right touch of depth to it.

"I sure am." I'm surprised by how calm my reply sounds. She bites her lip before continuing.

"Well then, follow me…"

We wind up a set of stairs to the top floor of the library. She keeps some distance while we're still in public spaces, but when we're alone in a quiet, dim hallway at the top, she turns with a conspiratorial grin, grabs my arm and slides it around her waist. We stop in front of a door, the wooden kind with a frosted glass window, and she fumbles with the keys for a minute. Inside are some stacked chairs, spare tables and dusty towers of boxes. The lights are off and the whole room has a kind of mauve tone from a skylight high above. She locks the door and slides her arms around me, bringing my face close as she inhales and shuts her eyes.

"We store old marketing stuff here. Nobody will come in. Probably."

And then I don't care if anyone comes because we're kissing; it's as slow, hot and perfect as I could have dreamed. I back her toward one of the massive tables and then lift her up onto it. Her feet playfully circle around my legs as I unbutton her blouse.

I don't know how long it lasts; it feels like it's slipping away, even as it happens. When it's over, I see her smile at my goofy grin as I get dressed.

"How do I look?" I ask. "You look happy."

"You look like you just got fucked."

I give a short laugh and then go silent, struck by how different her dry husky voice sounds from the gauzy purple tenderness I'm wrapped in inside.

The purple haze lingers into the afternoon. Sitting at my desk, I keep bringing my hands to my face to inhale the smell of her. Could we be like that again? Jesus, why didn't I ask her that before I left? I want to write her immediately. But then I think, don't be a schmuck, don't do it too soon - it looks desperate and needy. There are parts of the afternoon when I literally have to sit on my hands to resist the temptation to write, but somehow I make it through.

All through the restless night, I toss and turn with fitful, violet-tinged visions of the two of us in the storeroom.

VI: Holy Mother of God

Friday morning, I'm at work early. It's not like sleep was happening. Besides, the only thing I want to do is return to my computer, my connection to her. When I get to my desk, there's a blankness in the center of my head, like the bleak whiteness of a hangover. And yet I feel a buzz of excitement around that hollow core at the thought of writing to her. I go straight to my personal e-mail before opening my work account and start to type.

> *Have you ever...*
>
> *...done something where you wonder if it will be as good as you think it will be, and then it's even better? I was awake all night, thinking of running my hand over your smooth ivory shoulders, counting the freckles there. All I know is that I want to do it again. I look forward to seeing the look on your face when we're in the middle of our next misadventure.*

That's sweet, right? It ought to be. I changed every word in it at least twice. Aware that I need to work sometime today, I hit SEND. Now it's all about spreadsheets and waiting.

The waiting is mostly a matter of feeling mocked by the desultory numbers marring the pristine whiteness of my screen. My e-mail only pings twice, once for a reminder about our book club meeting next week, and once for a monthly newsletter from the local archdiocese. Then late in the morning comes a message titled *"Thank You"*. I hold my breath as I open it. The whole office seems to take on the hush of a snowfall.

Thanks for an awfully sweet message. I wanted to let you know that, while I enjoyed our time together, I'm not interested in doing it again. It's not because of you - you're adorable - and you should know that you smell amazing. It's simply that this once is all I'm comfortable with. Hope you understand.

Take care,

Mary

Now the hushed snowfall is more like a blizzard. The noise of the office swirls around me, and I blink back something that I tell myself cannot possibly be tears. I stand up from my desk and lurch toward the elevator; all I can think is that I have to get out, get away.

"Hey! Are you okay?"

Whipping around the corner with an inter-office envelope, Lourdes almost collides with me. Her round eyes make me wonder what I must look like.

"I'm… fine. Just need to get some air."

"Oh, okay. Take care!"

It's not her fault that I wince when she says the same words as Mary's sign-off. I feel a pang of regret at her pain as I board the elevator.

With a clenched jaw, I try to get my feelings under control on the ride down. I figure I can let them out once I get outside, but instead I walk as fast as I can. Putting downtown behind me, I head in the direction of the ivory bulk of the Transamerica Pyramid. The steam in my head finally dissipates in the vicinity of Washington Square Park. I sit down on a bench after a cursory exam to make sure there's nothing sticky and dreadful on it.

I lean back and gaze at the whitewashed face of the cathedral across from the park. Stupid, it's all so stupid. Fluffy clouds scud by in the sky behind the church, and I wonder what the hell I was thinking. That this woman with a boyfriend, who was arranging to meet me on the side, was going to have feelings for me?

Iridescent pigeons flock and scatter around the park in gray, green, blue and white. My recollections pretty much do the same: The icy drop in my stomach at the message from Mary this morning. Her face glowing across the bar that first night a week ago, an unexpected glimpse of the kind of promise that never seems to come my way. I remember the heady rush of each message I opened, and the near delirium of meeting her at the café. And yet, like some sycophantic tool, I feel cheered even now that she said I smelled nice.

Holy Mother of God, is that really what I want? Running around with someone else's girlfriend? Being blown off after that ridiculous, tacky scene in the storeroom? I shake my head and stand. I've had enough of what fantasy turns into. It's time to get back to work.

VII: Pray For Us Sinners

A few months later, I'm straining uphill on a crisp December evening, grit crunching on the sidewalk under my shoes as my breath billows into crystalline clouds in the darkness. Pete from my book club is having a holiday party at his place. It's the first time I've been there, and it will be good to see the rest of the crew too. We've had trouble scheduling a follow-up to our last book, some thousand page tome that was sort of sci-fi, sort of not and full of clever fake footnotes.

I also thought it would be a good chance for Lourdes to meet some of my friends.

"Are you sure they're going to like me?"

"If there's a person who wouldn't like you, I don't want to meet them."

She slides into ridiculously heart-warming dimples, and slips a black-mittened hand into mine. We've been together for about a month, and this is one of our first social appearances as a couple. I truthfully can't imagine anybody there not liking her; I'm actually more worried what she'll make of the host. Pete is a heck of a guy, but he's also an outspoken Republican. To my delight, Lourdes has turned out to be passionately Liberal. I'm fairly sure, though, that their mutual charm will win out over their potential oil and water political mixture.

We let ourselves in the gate and go through an ivy-lined brick courtyard. Bright cheer beckons inside, and we get caught up in a whirlwind of introductions as soon as we enter. Some of the people are from the book club; a lot are friends of his that I don't recognize. Someone tells us that Pete and the drinks are in the kitchen.

We make our way through to the pleasant, white-tiled oasis crowded with people in different knots of discussion. Pete presides in the center over a wooden-topped island counter crowded with libations. He breaks into a grin and waves a big hand when he sees me.

"Hey there! Glad you could make it."

"Yeah, thanks for the invitation." I introduce Lourdes and Pete to each other, and tell her that he's a great guy.

"This guy here is a great guy too. A little mushy-headed politically with all that liberal nonsense, but otherwise really solid." She swallows a giggle and gives me a sidelong smile. "Hey man, I don't think you've ever met my girlfriend. Let me introduce you guys. Hey, honey!"

Oh God. She's wearing a black crushed velvet dress, her back to me, but I recognize her even before she turns around. Mary. Shit, she said her boyfriend was named Peter. And I knew his girlfriend worked in some kind of job for the city. But never once did all these facts assemble themselves in one place in my head. Her eyes go wide when she turns to see me, but then she covers it with a smile that probably only I know is a little too tight.

I think we do a very passable simulation of a first meeting. While our quartet makes small talk, I look at Pete's big sunny grin and see the silent pleading in her eyes. I realize he doesn't know. Not just about me in particular, but that she does the kind of thing we did. They don't have an arrangement, they never did. I need some space. It takes me a shamefully short amount of time to come up with a pretext. I draw Lourdes off to one side.

"Hey, I just remembered. I forgot to call my parents back earlier about holiday travel plans. I'm going to run outside and do it. Be back in a minute."

"Are you worried about leaving me alone?" She laughs that husky laugh that I'm coming to love. "Don't sweat it, I'll be fine with Mr. Conservative." She pulls me in for a quick kiss.

Out in the courtyard, I tilt my head back and stare up at the narrow strip of sky. The icy diamond pinpricks and the obsidian infinity behind them seem like a judgment, a rebuke. This is awful.

Pete, and Lourdes here. What am I going to do? I've got to get my head clear, figure out—

I hear the creak of the front door open and then shut again. When I look back, Mary's there, hands wrapped around her body to protect against the coldness of the night. The sense memory of my arms around her comes back to me with a sudden vividness.

"God, I feel awful about this."

"It's fine." But the set in my jaw says different. This is her fault, her lies. And I'm still mad at her, mad all over again at being cast aside. Mad at myself that I thought I could get my hands on what I wanted, but it wasn't there.

"You need to know that I didn't tell the truth. Back then. Peter doesn't—"

"I know."

"So you aren't going to…?" She trails off, and I can see the fear in her eyes. As upset as I am, I know it's worse for her. I knew there was a boyfriend, knew she wasn't really mine. She is his, though, and she has a lot more to lose here than I do.

"No. I don't want to make any trouble for you. And I sure as hell don't want to try to explain it to anyone here tonight."

"Thank you."

She brushes her hand down my arm before turning to go back in. I watch her slip inside and then return to gazing at the darkness above.

So she's a sinner. And I'm a sinner, a fool on top of it for thinking that I'd find something real in all that cyber-pursuit and rushed tryst in the storeroom. But she has someone inside that warm glow coming through the window from the living room. And there's a real connection, or at least a shot at it, waiting for me there too. Maybe it is okay. Maybe somebody prays for all of us sinners, and there's mercy for us.

Now and at the hour of our death.

Prince Charming

Shannon Yashcheshen

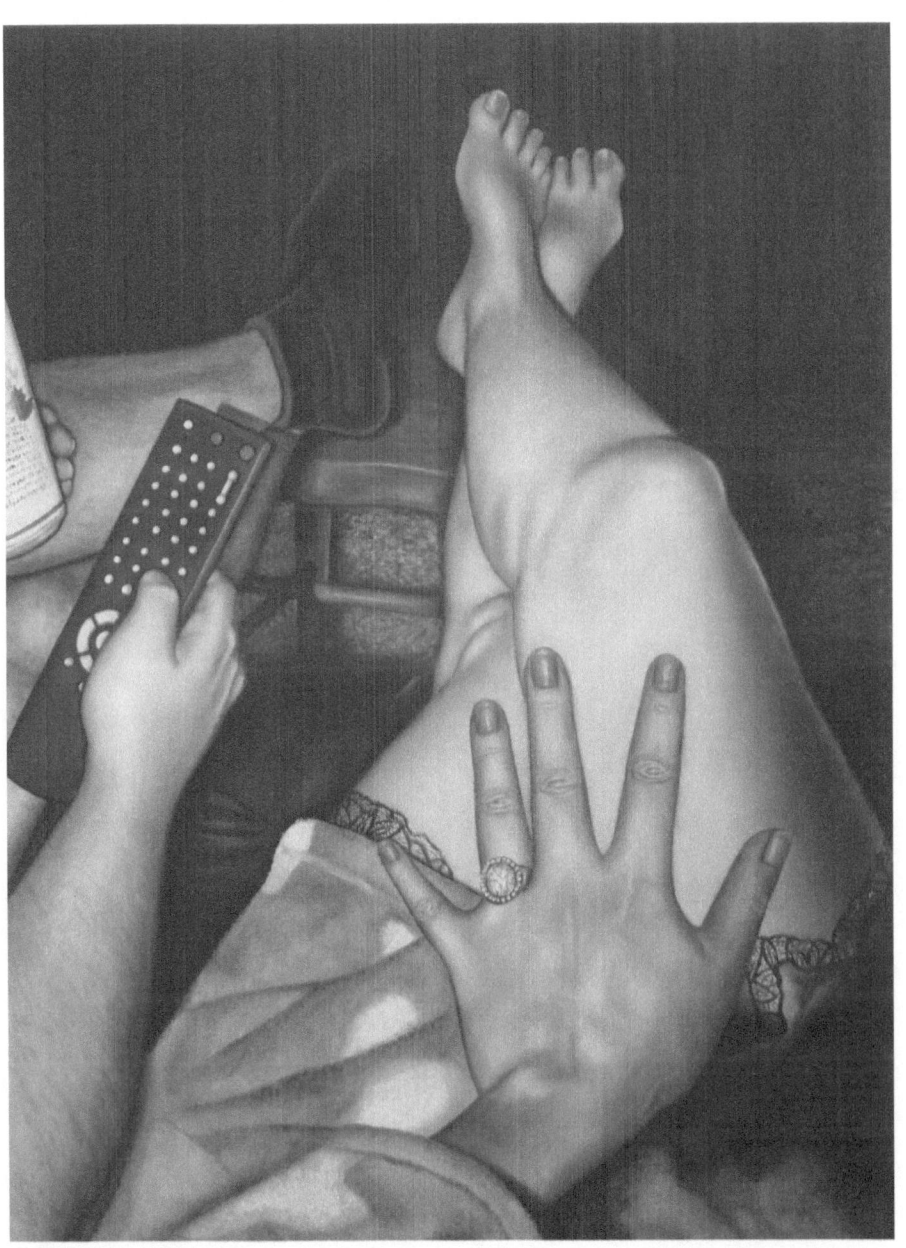

The Answer

Elynne Chaplik-Aleskow

"What do you want in your life that you do not have?" he asked me.

I thought about that question being open to whatever I might feel was the answer. I had everything I wanted except for one possibility. The answer to this question was something only I knew. It was personal and profound and private. It was a thought that had intrigued me since I had started to read about the animal world.

I looked at him, locking my eyes with his. Neither of us blinked for a long time. We sat in silence.

I knew that I delighted in being a woman, a lover, a friend. I relished where I lived and what I did with my time. I took pleasure in loving my partner and being loved by him.

Yet there was something that had never left me since I first learned about it. It fascinated me and challenged me so deeply that I decided it was my only answer to the question.

" Have you ever heard of a protogynous hermaphrodite?" I asked.

"No," he answered.

"A protogynous hermaphrodite is an animal that begins its life cycle as a female. As the animal ages, based on internal or external triggers, it shifts sex to become a male animal. Many fish, such as the gag grouper, undergo just such a metamorphosis. Male fecundity increases greatly with age, so it makes sense to start off as a female and then turn into a male."

"Are you gay?" he asked.

"No," I answered. "I am not gay. I am not a transvestite. I do not feel I was born the wrong gender."

His eyes were glued to me. He seemed mesmerized.

"I would like to use my life experience and insight to live my life first as a female and then to evolve naturally like a protogynous hermaphrodite into a male. Having lived my life as a woman, I am willing to make myself into a male I can respect."

He seemed confused.

"Being the best woman I can be is a natural transition to the empathy needed to become the best male I can be," I said. My tone openly expressed my incredulity that he did not seem to understand what seemed obvious to me.

"This is the remaining wish of my life. I want to live as one gender and then by natural evolution, I want to experience being the other gender."

"In order for our scientists to grant your wish, you must expound further on the value of your request," he responded. "Scientifically all things are possible. You must articulate the core focus of your wish."

"What better way to be what I think a male should be than to understand what it is to be female. I would know and understand the needs and sensitivities of being a woman and the perspective of what type of male I would want to become. These realities are intertwined. They are the fabric of the same outcome."

He seemed a bit lost. "The fabric of the same outcome?" .

"Yes. As a woman, I understand what being female means. At the same time, I know what type of male I appreciate. Therefore, in this evolution from one gender to another, I would know how to act as a man in relating to women and in fulfilling my humanity."

Now he was smiling at me as though he was beginning to understand.

"I would like you to place me in a society where this gender evolution is the norm. I would like to live among others who experience the value of knowing what it is to be both female and male and to use the wisdom of age."

"I understand your request. I will have an answer for you in a week."

Walking home, I wondered how I would tell my lover and my family about my plan. This certainly would come as a shock. Yet I felt completely at peace with my wish. It was a concept that utterly fascinated me. How wondrous to live naturally as both genders. I could use my life experience as being the best woman I knew how to be to become the best man I wanted to be. I could better understand varied points of view and verbal and non-verbal communication differences. I had a delicious fashion sense for men's clothing and loved the thought of dressing in a completely different gender. Mixing colour and pattern schemes of shirts and ties was such an enjoyable idea to me. It would be great fun to express my maleness through my fashion sense.

I had great confidence in my ability to deal with my change in gender communication and dress. I also had great comfort in my gender dancing skills and friendship capacity.

That left sports and sex. I knew that I would never be a great female or male athlete. Yet so much of male communication and bonding was based on sports. I knew that I would have to become competent in at least one physical activity. Working out at the gym would probably be my answer, much as it had been as a female.

As I had been as a female, I would be a male who loved the arts. Theater, film, and music would continue to be great interests. These thoughts filled me with excitement and made me more hopeful to have my wish granted and implemented.

Sex was the one area I wanted to give great consideration. I loved sex because I had a gentle and talented partner. Being a woman, I certainly knew what made sex successful for me. I also knew what my partner wanted and enjoyed. The physical gender changes would be the greatest challenge I would face in this evolution.

Yet the most important part of my communication and sexual skills as a future male would be my ability to empathize and to live in a male/female partnership in which both of us were fulfilled emotionally, intellectually and physically. This is what I experienced as a woman and is what I would recreate as a man.

I had a successful career. I experienced deep love and friendship. I had enough money to do what I wanted in my lifetime. And now I wanted it all. I wanted to be a human protogynous hermaphrodite. I wanted the experience of beginning life as a female and the new challenges of evolving into a male.

In one week, I would receive my answer. In one week, I would know if science would create for humans what was a natural cycle in part of the animal kingdom.

The key was the aging process. The foundation of my evolution would be the experience, empathy and resulting insights of my gender herstory as I transformed into my new gender history.

First Born

Matt Jones

So often in life, you end up spending twelve years in Kansas when you only intended on it being two. Then you leave and wonder where you went and where you can find the same stagnantly high levels of self-deprecating devotion to a similar six square miles of dead soil rife with working-class poor, erectile dysfunction, and sexually inhibited wives so devoutly attached to their men that they'd as soon as rest their chins on the exploding end of a twelve gauge with twitchy fingers before badmouthing their husbands for inadequate half chubs and arthritic joints over morning coffee.

You leave a place like Kansas and when you drive away, the day's dying rays of the sun let go of your car and your drive so that you may never have to look back.

Then you head east.

You are on your way to Volga. This is in West Virginia, but the people here do not seem to know it. It is a place teeming with sexually explicit children whose faces, upon slurring strands of vulgarity, pan off into the mist that hangs over the many mountains in anticipation of some great reprimanding.

"Do you know what that word means?"

Their minds stir with the same impetus of water buffalo that satisfy their thirst while staring into the banks of tepid and murky water, awaiting the crushing force of reptilian jaws and teeth that act so efficiently in filleting meat from bone. It is not too far from the way in which an adolescent boy pushes the mower over the entrails and stained fur of a blind and unfortunate marsupial.

You gather all of this quickly upon arriving in Philippi on the I-119 and learning that almost all the pancakes are made from cornmeal.

A boy whose pores leak Mountain Dew and a forehead stained tan with the stink that surely stuck because of dried fish scales under his fingernails scowls at you in a manner that neither of you understands.

You say, "Do you know about Kentucky?"

He does not reply and instead appears scrawny and weak, Yet you can imagine that he is adept with a hunting knife and has never learned to appreciate or obsess about his penis in the way that a normal boy should.

A waitress, presumably his mother, walks by; you know then that the entire town is related.

You roll a pancake into the shape of a cigar and pretend to smoke it; you begin to wonder if this is actually a restaurant or just someone's home.

There are no stray cats. You want to smell his breath, put your ear close to his clammy skin and malnourished paunch and listen for meows.

"Are you hungry?" you ask.

You take a drag from the flapjack and tilt your head backward. The lighting of the room gives his face a strange twitch and the sense that only the most diabolic residents have learned how to smile. His teeth show just enough to suggest that he subsists on handfuls of raspberry preserves or raccoon parts. It must be the lighting.

Upon leaving, you hand the waitress a napkin that says "Napkin" and walk over to the boy; you give him a seashell that you found in the shower of a motel in Savannah. No soap. Climbing into your car, you examine the outside of the building; the windows are spotless and there is no mailbox.

* * *

"Each fetus festers inside them like a tapeworm might inside the intestine of a feral dog until the day that the body takes care of itself."

Who said this to you? You know you heard it somewhere.

* * *

Certain cultures have dads and others have fathers.

Your father was a dad and his father was a father, so it was understandably difficult for him to move away from that role--your dad--not his father.

The distinction can be made between the two by how much emphasis is placed on the land, that or their responsiveness to amateur tambourine. It might sound crazy, but it is only something a dad could understand.

Your dad lived in Volga with his father and a slew of brothers and sisters who did not care and would never care to know about carbonation, or the state of an unincorporated town that couldn't find itself on a map. It was the same then as it is now.

*   *   *

The ridges in the clouds are smooth and rich like old dairy and puffs of smoke, creamy thighs with sets of dirty fingerprints and smudges of incest.

Volga—A city without consent.

Where the I-119 meets the 11 seems like the perfect place to build a church, or maybe even found a new religion. A landscape composed of masses of trees so boundless that it is stifling to step out of the sun and into the shade. The tree line should never be that prominent.

A couple of miles into the 11, you see the boy from Phillippi. He is walking southbound, shoulders with the deep red texture that one might find in splotches on the skin of a peach.

You pull up next to him and are not so sure it is him anymore.

"Are there more of you?" you ask.

All the children here appear as if they have spent one too many hours in Sunday school, a Sunday classroom where they suffer the abuse of an old, taut woman who has never been touched, drunk hard liquor or acquired a cat.

Because there are no churches.

There are no stray cats.

"The fetuses fester."

Who was it who said that?

"Would you like a ride to where you are going?"

"The fetuses fester."

The boy whispers this with his head out the window, eyes squinting into the sun as you cruise down the uneven road.

You move to turn on the FM dial, but are worried it might spook him. The bones in his back writhe under his skin while his head rests on the edge of the window, small droplets of drool sucked along his cheek by the warm funnel of air.

You drive for almost an hour before deciding that he simply has nowhere to go. You let him sleep off the exhaustion that has surely come from a full day of chasing hares and wrestling hounds.

*　　*　　*

Your mother and your grandfather, your dad's father, made love once before and had sex many times after that—sex that made pelvic bones collide like battling musk oxen, grinding into a fine dust that piled beneath their feet and filled with a pool of sweat like a mashed potato volcano might with gravy.

*　　*　　*

"You will want to father these children. That is just how it is. You will want to father them until you realize that they too will grow beards and thick forearms and the lust that is so common with the men of the mountains. You will want to father them when they are young, lithe, weak and wandering the roads near death. This, however, is when they no longer need to live."

Your dad said this to you. Or his father said it to him, and he said it to you, not in his own words, but how he was once told it. You're not sure.

"You will want to save them and grow them up strong. Instead, lay their limp bodies somewhere cool, somewhere outside the stench of the sun, so they can rest."

It must have been his father.

"Their fetuses fester."

That could have been him too. Your father, not his dad.

*   *   *

You don't see a station for a while and park alongside the road to rest your eyes. Upon waking, the sun is still high in the sky.

You don't know any of their names; it's not even that it's hot, just bright.

"They don't even know their names."

You say that.

The colours of everything fade beneath the white light; deep and brilliant greens look transparent in the distance, leaves peeling off like strips of old paint that burst into the wind and crumble into shattered light. Dead stars and weak flames disappear into the air in such silence that once the trees are dry and branches bare, you wonder what spring looks like.

Volga—Cataract capital of the world.

It feels like that--looking through cataracts. It feels like feeling old.

It's that same sun--bright. It falls from the sky like a flash-bang and engulfs the terrain in a sharpness that skews the horizon into something that sits right in front of your face.

*   *   *

When you stop in Pryse, you learn that no one there really calls it Pryse anymore. They refer to it as Old Genoa, most likely not due to heritage or old money, but more so because of a mispronunciation, some Italian they strung up, or a salami wrapper they found caught in the branches where they strung up some Italian. Irony is out of reach in Old Genoa.

You spend a week there before heading east to Volga. You hadn't intended on staying more than a night, but upon returning for the first time in so many years, you feel compelled to catch up with those who are still around.

The girls whom you had spent so many nights with seem no more like women, except for the wrinkles that creep across their foreheads and the depth in which their eyes sink, their breasts still small and timid beneath thick layers of fabric that catch and trap body heat, turning it into sweat, doubt and stench.

Two in particular—Michelle and Mary—have been married for some time since you left, mothers to six children between them: two small girls with faces speckled by freckles and dimwittedness as well as four boys, three of which are too small to be yours. One, however, is lean and tall, probably twelve years old. His name is Jacob, like so many others. Jacob, the first.

Jacob came from a night that you had spent with Mary, one fueled by some mechanical yearning that suggested you do it simply for the sake of doing. She cried into your chest once before and once after, the first time in fear and the second time in what she professed to be love. Her underdeveloped hips had trouble adjusting to the breadth of your frame. You tilted your head all the way back, so you could stare upside down at a stack of rotten beams while she wiggled on top of you. When it was over, when she sobbed, you stayed for six more days.

Looking at Jacob now, still a full foot shorter than yourself, you are sure he is one of your own. His body is strong and sleek, dotted with dirt, grime and waxy muscle that shifts under the heat of the sun. He spends most of the day outside with his father, a bearded man whose face is interchangeable with so many others. You stay for six more days.

Mary and Michelle do not recognize you and this makes it easier.

As with most of your journey eastward, there are just so many children - walking along the roadways, in and out of the woods, running in packs - small footprints that kick up dust into the air and the lungs. Yet almost no one is old.

This is how you would do it:

You would take Jacob in your car with you to show him a place that was too far to walk. He would tell you that he had walked further than anyone could imagine. You would tell him that you imagined this to be true, then ruffle his hair, and catch sight of yourself in the way he ground his teeth in displeasure. You would drive him about thirty miles into Big Doe Creek, into the part where the water was at its widest. You would park the car and bring him to the water. And when he was consumed by the sound of it running, by the complete lack and presence of life all at once, you would do it.

This is how you do it:

Upon climbing into your car, you close your eyes and cradle his thin throat in a grip so tight that your palms burn later. You lay his nimble body in the backseat and drive away, forcing a smile and a wave to Mary and two small girls. You drive for over two hundred miles before pulling off to the side of the road to look at him. After that, you drive for two more days before it starts to smell. After that, you lay his body in the woods somewhere just outside of Hamlin.

*   *   *

You know that when your mother was a young girl, she met your dad. And you know that when your dad met your mother, she also met his father.

"Your mother and I did not have the chance that many young lovers hope for."

You know he never spoke with such eloquence, but it gave you a sense of clarity to remember it that way. Instead of spittle, liquor, drool and a stuttering rage, it is better for you to know it this way.

"I did not have the chance that I needed."

You are sure he said this in such a way that did not sound like testimony, but rather a dreary acknowledgement of the way things were, are and would be.

*   *   *

Crossing the West Virginia state line, you call your wife from a payphone inside a motel run by a man who sputters to a start each day, simply by realizing that if he does not run the motel, no one will. Then he lies in bed for a minute more, eyes fixated on a ceiling with a watermark that has slowly spread into the shape of nothing at all; he wonders if anyone will come to his motel that day. After a minute more, he drifts back into sleep again and dreams of people and places that he can't rightly recall ever knowing or visiting. After that, he wakes up with his mind at ease because he is no longer tired and must alleviate his shriveling bladder. And after that, you come in to use the payphone.

"Good afternoon, nice day, isn't it?"

He says, "I suppose it is."

You slide in some change and tell your wife that you are in West Virginia. She asks how things are.

"They are great," you say.

She agrees that she is great as well.

You tell her that you must go because you have a lot of driving to get done.

She asks how he is doing.

"He is old and sick. It is hard to say until I get there."

He is a sick, old man.

"Well," she says, "I'm sure he will be glad to see you.

"I love you."

"I do love you."

You hang up.

The man behind the counter tells you that he misses his wife sometimes.

"Where is she?" you ask.

He tells you that he does not know - off with friends, he supposes.

His eyes are glazed with a cracked film of milky white that you delicately peel off and lay on the counter.

He blinks at you twice and says, "Welcome to West Virginia. It's almost heaven."

"Yes," you say, "Almost."

He ponders this a moment more and agrees with you.

The next day, his motel does not open, but the payphone is used twice.

You walk out of the store and the breeze feels as clean and cool as ever. Upon stepping into your car, you tilt the rear view mirror and examine your flaccid penis in the reflection before driving away. It is disappointing in presentation.

In twenty-seven words, you try to sum up the purpose of your life. You struggle with sentence structure and adjective strings as well as ways to begin and end. Last year's twenty-six proved to be challenging, but you accomplished it, just as you did with twenty- five the year before, and twenty-four the year before that.

This year, sitting on the hood of your car, the sky folding into itself off in the distance, a swirl of lipstick, sand and glowing limestone, you struggle to compose yourself. You think of Jacob and the others, but Jacob especially. You wonder if he could be included in the twenty-seven. You wonder why the writing is always harder to do with more years and more words, always harder to dredge out the deeper meaning underneath a continuously growing pile of surface material.

"I am a man who has owned two dogs, one male and one female, and have done my best to learn how to cook."

That is from a few years ago. You wonder when things got so complicated.

*   *   *

Your wife was pregnant for almost six months. After that, you had a hard time. She smelled rotten and you'd stopped having sex. She knew where your family was from. You told her your mom and father had died.

Another six months after that, you'd gotten word that your dad's father was sick. You had always known him to be sick, but in this case, he was dying. He had sired enough children to commence the takeover of a small municipality, a fleet of incapable infantry that would more likely bite at the flanks and cuffs of men's pants before standing and fighting with their own two fists.

You knew yourself to be perhaps the only living relative who cared enough to see him go, to witness the unraveling of a man composed solely of flaws interwoven so tightly that one might mistake him for an intricately constructed soul instead of just a glamorous shell. You knew that he had taken a special interest in your dad; it was   developed just for the sake of the challenge and converted into a lifestyle and the death of a potentially good man and the birth of a potentially good son.

"I am growing up now and like it so far."

That was at ten.

After hearing about his illness, it was easy to go east. After crossing into Morganfield, it was easier to make a stop in Old Genoa. And after that, it was routine to spend a night or two in Crystal, Leeco, and Patsey, even though Patsey was out of the way. It's always good to catch up on old times.

More often than not, they are still there - the towns, that is. Occasionally, you find out that the people have gone; the women have left for other things or passed away from an illness that was entirely curable, if not preventable. The kids sometimes stayed around, but it was just so hard to tell. In Old Genoa, you knew there was only one child. However, there were always so many in other places, sometimes entire towns of children who seemed to be void of mothers or fathers, moms or dads.

In cases such as those, you identify all the ones who are of age and take them with you to the water. You are tired at the end of the day; the cords in your arms ache, are hot and feel like snapping, but you find time to bathe in the running water and dry in the open air before dozing off in the front seat. In the morning, you gather the rest of the little ones and tell them about composing yourself in a certain number of words.

To that, they say things like:

"I am tired."

"I am hungry."

"Who are you?"

All true.

To that, you reply, "Surely all of you are not three."

You leave each town, each gathering of people big enough to constitute a meaningful geographical place with its own culture, values, and rules instead of just an area built on happenstance, lust, and an inconceivably underdeveloped awareness of birth control. You leave knowing that each of them will grow older and probably never learn to count. You leave knowing that many of them probably share the same lineage and will continue to share other aspects of themselves that should not be shared in such a way.

"Do you know what is out there, beyond all of this? Don't any of you ever wonder what there is when you leave this place?"

You ask them this before leaving with a hint of frustration in your voice.

"More of us?"

"Something like that," you say.

You ask yourself the same question when driving away and know that there is nothing beyond this place for them. It does not matter what is outside of this place, whether it is cities, strip malls or strip clubs, because there is no way to escape the state of mind fostered from within the dense tree lines and unincorporated townships, to escape the time cultivated from within mothers who know nothing about the joy of birth and everything about the indifference of living without really knowing it to be that.

Volga—It's a state of mind.

Yes, it is.

When you finally arrive in Volga, the air is thick and moves through you slowly like bitter maple sap. The wind plays piano notes that are out of tune and strained by incapable fingers, notes that are sucked through the breeze and collapsed into the blowing like a woman's scream might be sucked into a black hole and wrung into scattered bits of sobbing and hysterical laughter. You try to speak, to hear the sound of your own voice, but your words are languid and spill out of your mouth in great drops that splatter onto the ground and splash onto your shoes.

I'm here, you think.

Volga is not so much a town as just a home - one that acquired the means to feed enough mouths so that one might consider it a population instead of a family.

You park your car on a gravel path that winds its way up to a house with a face that sags, a foundation exhausted from the wear of muddy footprints and bitter winters.

A swarm of children traipse across the yard, the open space, dirt kicking up into the air and the lungs. Women patter around the property, a dull drone of broken grass blades drowned out by the rustling of dry leaves and expulsion of phlegm from inside the house.

You know all of them are you, and yourself, all of them, and make peace with that before going inside.

Afterwards, you swim through the sound of the phlegm to the front door, a torn screen that shutters in the thick breeze. Inside, the floorboards are lined with age and dust. The couches are waterlogged and many curtains hang over window frames that hold no glass.

You take the familiar steps back down the main hall; it grows narrower with each step forward. You follow the sound of booming phlegm and the feel of the spread of sickness that makes its way from your heart to the tips of your fingers. Itt is a sickness that all dogs must know when they are called upon by men who would as soon stroke their flanks and smile as nestle inside their warm bodies after slicing through their soft underbellies.

And once that sickness reaches the tips of your toes, nails fading to a brittle black that flakes off inside your shoes, you stop at the door and put your hand on the knob.

"Is that you out there?" he calls.

His words trickle through the gaps in the crooked door frame and scurry up your pant leg and into your innards like a rat trying to escape a hot tin.

Upon opening the door, you see his weak body propped up in bed, his skin a pale gray mound of blank expression that bunches up at the eyes.

He smiles and coughs, then coughs again and says he is glad you came.

You stand in the doorway and make note of the cool draft in the room. You observe that his feet are bare. The sickness in your gut has climbed its way up your spine and into the crow's nest inside your head, the one built from sticks, candy wrappers, cotton fiber and a lifetime of misunderstanding that trickles through you and evaporates off your skin like raindrops from a spider web.

He asks if you have seen your mother.

Your hands shake and you say yes.

And your brothers and your sisters, he asks.

All of them, you say.

The air is still around you both. No laughter emanates from the outside, no fragmented, black hole shrieking, sobs or pattering across the yard.

He lifts himself with a great deal of effort from his bed and walks over to the window to pull back the curtain. Upon opening it, you see his knees twitch as he stares outside at what would soon be cooked into a pungent stew by the summer sun.

You think of the old man at the motel, what old age looked like and what young faces feel like resting in the open palm of your hand. You think about calling your wife and all the still, soil-stained lips lying so ornately across the yard.

He turns to you and asks about the baby.

"Each fetus festers inside them like a tapeworm might inside the intestine of a feral dog until the day the body takes care of itself."

He tilts his chin and pulls his eyes inward, gazing upon you with genuine interest, the skin under his eyes tinted yellow and tarnished with grease. It's in our blood, he says.

He pulls back the curtain once more and peeks outside.

He tells you to get out there and clean up before it starts to stink.

Your arms are already tired, the grip in your hands lost to the delicate, fingerprinted and struggle-stained necks in front of the house.

You close the door behind you and walk back down the hall and out into the yard.

You kneel down next to a golden, ruffled head of hair, a chili bowl chest with narrow shoulders, thin lips still pink with life, so moist they might touch once more and speak. You lay down in the damp dirt, cool from the cold buried so far beneath it—unreachable and ancient--and rest your head upon his empty stomach, a cavern to hold the last of the warmth that huddles in a mass, a small galaxy of dust and particles at the base of the sternum.

"Do you know about Kentucky?"

The space inside his flesh, the last of the warmth rising and evaporating like sweet steam, echoes hollow.

I do, you say.

You stare out into sloping hills that end abruptly in trees hiding a sun that slinks away from what it has seen each day. You turn your gaze west, so far off into the distance that everything you know sits itself on the tip of your nose and the man inside barks phlegm.

Volga—There's no place like home.

This Scheme For Perpetual Peace Is Very Interesting, But Hardly Feasible

Cat Manolis

Contributor Bios

Julianna Kozma – Beautiful Insanity

Julianna Kozma is the author of two novels for young adults: Mosquitoes of Summer, and Secrets of the Dunes. She was a financial journalist for 15 years and wrote for several international publications before breaking into the book publishing world after winning the 2009 Book Idol contest. She is also a fulltime contract teacher, in both elementary and high school.

Gerard Lange – Memorial Tree No. XIV

Trained in the areas of sculpture, drawing and photography Gérard Lange's artwork tends to be as diverse as his background. Lange worked professionally as a photographer before attending graduate school at Tulane University in New Orleans. After receiving his MFA, Lange taught at Northern Michigan University then Barton College in Wilson, North Carolina where he now resides. Despite his profession as a professor of photography, Lange works in whatever media he sees fit for a particular project. Most often he employs a wax and wane between traditional media and photography, coupled with digital imaging, as well as sculpture. Lange has had numerous exhibitions both nationally and internationally and his work has been featured in a variety of publications and journals. Additionally, Lange has delivered numerous lectures on his work and the history of photography, is represented by galleries in New Orleans, New York and London and his work is held in several public and private collections of note.

Keith Kennedy – Teeth as Eyes saw Aida, Unafraid

Keith Kennedy has published short fiction in Nocturnal Ooze, Midnight Times, Aurora Wolf, Anotherealm and Bete Noir, as well as the Aurora Rising Anthology. He's published poetry in Niteblade, Heroic Fantasy Quarterly, Kindling, the Poetic Pinup Revue and A Handful of Stones. Recently nominated for the Pushcart Prize and the Rhysling Award, he will be published in the SFPA's anthology of the best poetry of the year. Keith lives in Vancouver with his wonderful wife, Nancy. Check him out daily at askkeithanything.blogspot.com.

David Hunter – Untitled

Born in 1968 in Ottawa, Ontario David graduated from the Fine Arts program at the Ontario College of Art, studied with the British Institute or Florence and Concordia University, and enjoyed a stint as medieval art restorer for the Bargello Museum of Florence, Italy.

He is currently working as a freelance designer and consultant for such high profile clients as The LCBO, Coca-Cola, The Environmental Commissioner of Ontario and The United Way.

David has exhibited his work with The Ward-Nasse Gallery in New York City, Galleria Villa Rosa in Florence, Italy and The White House Gallery in Toronto.

Andrea Beça – The Disappearing Act

Andrea Beça is a freelance writer, editor, playwright, and dramaturg, as well as Artistic Director of Cowardly Kiss Theatre. She currently resides in Edmonton, Alberta with her two dogs, Oscar Wilde Beça and Lucille Ball Beça.

Steve Wade – In Fields of Butterfly Flames

A prize nominee for the PEN/O'Henry Award, 2011, Steve Wade's fiction has been published widely in print and online. His work has won awards and been placed in prestigious writing competitions, including First Prize in the UK abook2read Literary Competition, and Second Place in the International Biscuit Publishing contest, 2009.

Katie Monahan – With Child

Katie Monahan, (born Detroit, MI) graduated from the University of Notre Dame in 2007 with a B.F.A. in Studio Arts degree. Now living in Los Angeles, she has gone on to develop a bold figurative style of painting highlighted in her complex murals and dynamic narratives. Working out of her private studio on the West Side, she continues to experiment with paint and textures while showing her work in fine art venues across Southern California as well as in private homes in locations around the world including: London, Belgium, Australia, Tahiti, Canada, Washington D.C., New York, LA, and more.

John Brooke – The Wife of Moby Dick

Montreal-based writer John Brooke has published four novels and several short stories. He has won the Journey Prize and a CBC-Quebec short fiction prize. His most recent book, Stifling folds of love - An Aliette Nouvelle Mystery, was published by Signature Editions, Winnipeg in Dec 2011. More info at http://www.aliette.ca

Emily Ursuliak – Cocoon

Emily Ursuliak is one part poet, one part novelist, two parts brandy; shake over ice, strain and serve with a slice of strange; garnish with small town innocence and add metropolitan excess to taste. She is currently pursuing a Masters of Arts in English with a creative writing thesis (her first novel) at the University of Calgary. She is also the artistic director of The Poetry Prowl: a roaming poetry festival in Red Deer, Alberta.

Chris LaMay-West – Ave Maria

Chris LaMay-West believes in the power of rock music, Beat poetry, and the sanctity of Star Trek. He has appeared in Kitchen Sink and Morbid Curiosity, in various online venues including the online edition of Opium, and in the Mortified reading series. A California native, Chris currently resides in Salem, Massachusetts, where he writes and lives with his lovely bride and two cats. His exploits, literary and other, can be followed at: http://chris-west.blogspot.com/.

Shannon Yashcheshen – Prince Charming

Shannon Yashcheshen is a graphic/web designer, painter, printmaker and photographer. She is originally from Yorkton/Regina, Saskatchewan, but now lives and works in Winnipeg, Manitoba. She has been an active member of the arts community for the past 13 years, is a member of several art galleries and art organizations, has extensive experience exhibiting her work in art galleries, has been nominated for and has won several prestigious art and design awards, and has worked as a graphic/web designer for several large corporations. Shannon has completed the Graphic Art Production, New Media Communications, and the Applied Photography extension programs at the SIAST Wascana campus in Regina, Saskatchewan, a Bachelor of Fine Art Degree with a double major in painting and printmaking, and a Bachelor of Arts Degree with a specialization in art history, at the University of Regina. She completed these programs with distinction and has successfully completed them while working full time as a graphic designer. Shannon is currently working on her Master of Fine Arts degree at the University of Manitoba, where she is completing advanced studies in painting, while training to be a studio art professor.

Elynne Chaplik-Aleskow – The Answer

Elynne Chaplik-Aleskow is a Pushcart Prize Nominated author and award-winning educator and broadcaster. She is Founding General Manager of WYCC-TV/PBS and Distinguished Professor Emeritus of Wright College in Chicago. Her adult storyteller program is renowned. Her stories and essays have been published in numerous anthologies including Thin Threads (Kiwi Publishing), Chicken Soup for the Soul (Simon & Schuster Distributor), This I Believe: On Love (Wiley Publishing), Forever Travels (Mandinam Press), Press Pause Moments (Kiwi Publishing), My Dad Is My Hero (Adams Media) and various magazines, including the international Jerusalem Post Magazine. Elynne's husband Richard is her muse. Visit http:// LookAroundMe.blogspot.com

Matt Jones – First Born

Matt Jones obtained his undergraduate degree in English from a small, liberal arts university in Austin, Texas. His work can be found in such publications as Forty Ounce Bachelors, Paper Darts, and Hoot Review. In the Fall of 2012, he will begin his MFA in Creative Writing at The University of Alabama with his trusty dog, Bagheera.

Cat Manolis – This Scheme For Perpetual Peace Is Very Interesting, But Hardly Feasible

Cat Manolis has exhibited and received awards for her art work nationally (U.S.). She received an M.F.A. in Sculpture, which probably explains her success in painting. As well as running her own design business, she lives in North Carolina, grows Habanero peppers and makes wicked hot sauce as self-diagnosed therapy.

Bev Sandell Greenberg – Volume Editor

Bev Sandell Greenberg is a Winnipeg writer and editor. Her short story is forthcoming in Prairie Fire and others have appeared in small Canadian and Amercan journals; her poetry has been featured on local transit buses. Bev's non-fiction publication credits include Living Legacies II, Herizons, Hard Jobbin', Mix Magazine, NeWest Review, Uptown, The Globe & Mail, The Winnipeg Free Press and Prairie Books NOW.

Ben Clarkson - Cover Art

Ben Clarkson is an artist and illustrator who currently resides in Winnipeg Manitoba. His work is often absurd and surreal. His illustrations have appeared across Canada in publications such as The Literary review of Canada and the Globe and Mail.

ZenFri Inc.

ZenFri Inc. creates and distributes cutting edge art & entertainment across a wide range of digital and traditional mediums. In an increasingly diverse media landscape, ZenFri boldly rethinks narrative conventions, merging mediums and technology in ways never before conceived, allowing our products to stand apart from the competition. Founded by Corey & Danielle King, a husband and wife duo seek to use traditional and digital frontiers to craft new ways of telling stories, spread innovative ideas, and explore the great circumstance we all find ourselves in.

Join Our Ranks

The best way to support *Warpaint* aside from reading it is to put yourself in the line of fire and submit your work. If you've ever had an idea your parents told you never to speak of again, or a painting deemed unsuitable for "polite society" send it our way. We may just publish it for all the world to see.

We're seeking bold, unusual and provocative work for the next battle in the war against conventional thinking, *Warpaint - Issue 2*. Due out at the end of the year.

Submit to Warpaint

We're now accepting submissions of your boldest, most unusual and provocative short fiction (up to 6000 words) and visual art for *Warpaint - Issue 2*. Take up arms against conventional thinking, enlist by submitting a work no later than August 31, 2012.

Previously published work and simultaneous submissions will be considered. By emailing us your work, you are agreeing to the Terms of Submission located at: zenfri.com/submissions.

Any files, questions or concerns about submitting may be sent to: submit@zenfri.com. We look forward to receiving your work.

www.ingramcontent.com/pod-product-compliance
Lightning Source LLC
Chambersburg PA
CBHW030516260626
47157CB00005B/1769